Tenets

A Lamentation's End
Novella

By Wade Lewellyn-Hughes

Front cover illustrated by Andrew Ryan
Copy Edits by Inspired Ink
Developmental Edits by Blue Falcon Editing
and F. Nicole Reynaud Peavey
ISBN-13: 978-0-9908175-2-9
ISBN-10: 0990817520

Published by Wisdom, Wonder & Whimsy Books

WWWBOOKS
Wisdom, wonder, & whimsy books

Dedication

For brothers, mine and yours.

Acknowledgments

Special thanks with your choice of dipping sauce to
Melanie, Shawn, and Nicole.
Extra special thanks to my mother and my wonderful husband, Bryce.

Contents

Liekelith

Aontus

Teallaigh Te

Gallaic Sea

Trône d'Argent

Racine

Chapter I: When in Aontus

Veen guided his two fellow mercenaries through the afternoon crowd passing between Aontus's port and the markets. At the dockside end of the Jervis Bridge, five little gurriers took turns rattling the bones and shouting the latest news. Veen waved for Elanis and Oren to follow him over to a filthy, pale boy. "What'd you say?" Veen asked.

The sight of a tawny-skinned Caperi stole the boy's tongue. Oren's creaseless eyes returned the gurrier's suspicion.

"Don't worry yourself, boy," Veen said. "The Caperi are friendly folk, even if they can't hold their drink like we real islanders do."

Oren crossed his arms over his leaf-beetle-shell vest.

The boy grinned before the other four behind him groaned at a knucklebone roll. He looked back to their game as he asked, "Prisoners escaped the Five Snakes?"

A bright-eyed boy rose next to him. "I said that. Take your turn, Fergus. He said . . ."

The second crier shouted, "Gone in the night with no trace, the missing lowlanders now number fourteen!"

"Missing lowlanders?" Veen asked. "Any folk from Teallaigh Te?"

The boy shrugged.

In threadbare clothes to see them through the chilly Lekelithian spring nights, the boys stirred memories of painfully cold toes and the taste of gurr cake on his tongue. Veen dropped a silver before each of them. "Youse get some new shoes and a pie, boys. Shoes first, yeah?"

Wide-eyed for the coin in his fingers, another gurrier halfheartedly shouted, "Albacore sunk between Aontus and Trône d'Argent. Nine Racinian nobles drowned."

"Good," barked a fisherman hauling his basket of tuna to the old market. Few Lekelithians believed the war was over or that the Racinian Empire would let their freedom stand, contrary to nearly ten years of peace.

"Veen," Elanis said through a fistful of her silver mantle. Its hood had been blown back, letting the drizzle sprinkle her spectacles. Her short black hair couldn't decide where to part as it rode the wind. "If we're to make ourselves tardier, may we do so away from the reek of the tanning yards?"

"Aye," Veen answered, waving her and Oren on. Wet sea winds pelted the filigree railings of the Jervis Bridge, named for the river below, and cleaned the stink of the prison's tanning yards from the air. Mostly.

Oren's golden-brown hand clasped Veen's shoulder. "This is your home? Explains your crooked smile. I can hear the cutpurses salivating."

With an inward sigh, Veen drew up to his full five-foot-two height. "'Tis just the spitting rain. Not ten years back, that was me, down to the shabby shoes. And I doubt they've seen a Caperi before."

"Oo," Oren agreed. "Speaking of shoes, what would Nelis say of your generosity back there?"

"Nothing," Veen said. "Never a more frugal soul has come out of Lekelith than my brother, but you've been fighting by our side long enough to know Nelis has a soft spot for wee ones, yeah?"

Oren thought and replied, "Mercifully, our assignments haven't involved many children."

Elanis released her mantle and peered over the bridge's railing. "I'm surprised to hear you think that is your older brother's soft spot," she added with a teasing grin. "You're sure we should leave Teague behind?"

A warehouse blocked the view of the wharf downhill, where Teague had received a chastising welcome home. Gleaming like the fire opals Teague's merchant father peddled, an arc of guards had insisted upon their leader's immediate return to his family estate.

At times like these, Veen very nearly thanked the gods his parents were long dead. "You don't want to sit there with a stiff lip while he gets scolded. And he told you to lead the meeting. And we're late, yeah? Let's strike off! I don't have to tell you the Towers wait for no man. Neither will Nelis when there's a paying job to be had." After hearing the news of missing lowlanders, Veen was far more eager to see his brother than meet with the mage who wanted to employ them. Nelis was fine. Surely.

Striding uphill into the old market, Veen set their path toward the green Tower of Aontus, the tallest building in the capital. After the successful revolution against the Racinian Empire, Lekelith's magi had converted the large round tower into a windmill, a new symbol for Lekelith, now finally free of war.

Veen pointed to it above the market. Perfectly timed, the sun broke free to shine through the four spinning amber sails. Veen smiled proudly. "There's the old Amber and Green, El."

"Now that is beautiful!" Elanis agreed.

The damp downtrodden scattered as soldiers parted the crowd for nobles who dared the alleys of the old market. Rich oil and common water never touched as they flowed along the muck-ridden streets.

Some commoner brutes sharpened their words for Elanis. Veen

and Oren flanked her. "I wish I had had time to change out of this dress," she said, blaming the ruby-red, wide-hipped gown she had needed for the Racinian court, but not her silver mantle.

More voices rose to demean the Racinian in their midst. Oren palmed the short axes lashed to his pack. Veen attempted the limb-breaking expression Nelis always wore before following through with a threat. The laughter thrown back at him said he and his two companions could use Nelis's muscle about now. Even one of the piks, waist-high men with broad noggins and large noses, belly-laughed at Veen's expense.

"Where is your brother?" Oren asked.

"Yes," Elanis said. "Between us, why didn't Nelis join us to Frysta Avfall?"

The question stirred Veen's concern. They'd never been apart this long before. "Ach. Youse know yourselves I got the same excuse Teague did."

Veen scanned the crowd in the old market again. High above the cloaked masses, one magpie stared down from the shelter of an overhang on the rooftops. One for sorrow.

"Well, whatever his reasoning," Elanis continued, "I hope he honors Teague's orders. This is my meeting. Frankly, I'm curious as to why a mage from the Tower of Aontus hired a band of the Hook. What could mercenaries achieve that his superiors could not? His grand diviner holds as much weight as Lekelith's council."

Past the last tavern spilling fiddled tunes, the three mercenaries breached an iron gate identifying the New Market District. Fine red brick had replaced the irregular cobblestones in the streets. Veen patted his belt to make sure his black steel daggers had stayed loyal to him.

Haberdasheries and jewelers filled in the absence of taverns and temples between the stalls. Veen breathed through his nose after getting a bitter mouthful of wafting perfume. Floral scents and bath powders overtook what whiffs remained of the tanning yard's stink.

Amber-colored mantles, identical in every way except color to Elanis's silver achievement, grew more common. The mages eyed Elanis with kinder suspicion than the commoners had.

"Shortcut," Veen said, ducking into another alleyway. Emerging from behind a fine leatherworks shop, they finally reached the Tower of Aontus's square. When the amber-filled sails swung low overhead, Veen felt the magic hum through his bones. He nodded up at the Tower. "Nelis told me once that the whole wharf could fit inside the old Amber and Green. Do you think so?"

"I very much doubt that," Elanis answered.

White-clad men and one woman protected the Tower's entrance. Spellbreakers. Silent monks. They weren't warriors, just eerie. Trained to resist magic's effects, their hard faces betrayed as much emotion as a snake's before the strike.

Elanis approached the podium next to the Tower's curved double doors. The paralibrarian on duty adjusted his amber mantle. "Oh, the thrill when a silver mantle from Trône d'Argent graces our presence," he said flatly to the spellbreaker at his side.

"So much for camaraderie through magic," Elanis mumbled. "We have an appointment with Mage Dreanen Curtiss."

Running a disinterested gaze over them, the paralibrarian paused on Veen. "Don't suppose you belong to that other boggytrotter?"

"Aye," Veen said gruffly, though his stomach settled some upon hearing Nelis had arrived. He turned to Elanis and Oren. "He means Nelis. Told youse he wouldn't wait."

"That was the name," the mage muttered, scanning his parchment. He let out a curt sigh. "Ye're late."

Elanis's ivory cheeks flushed. "Later by the minute. Give us directions or find someone amenable to assist us. I offer you that choice before I register a complaint with your librarian, your chronicler, and your archivist."

The paralibrarian's eyes narrowed at the threat.

"We are here as representatives of the Hook at the behest of your Mage Curtiss. Your actions very well may denigrate the reputation of your

Tower."

He ran a finger down the scroll before him. "Idealistic mercenaries? It doesn't say."

Elanis rubbed her forehead with her thumb. "Well I just did." Her temper was rising, a frightening thing in Elanis. Instead of losing control of her anger, she tended to lose her emotions, locking them away to become an icy being of rationality. Given that Nelis had now taken her meeting, the paralibrarian was unwittingly priming her for a larger fight.

"Yes," he replied, "though you could have said earlier. Third floor, right off the stairs, second study on the left."

Veen had been inside the Tower once as a boy when Nelis had dragged him there out of desperation to cure an outbreak of hives; he knew better than to accept those directions in good faith. "Which stairs?"

"East bank," the paralibrarian barely uttered. He waved them off.

Elanis gave the hem of her mantle a quick jerk beneath her bosom.

The spellbreakers parted and opened the Tower, bathing them in the familiar odor of peat fires. Seven thinner towers hid within. The old round tower's plethora of stairs created an intentional maze in the reconstructed interior.

"You know," Elanis uttered as she took it all in, "I may have been wrong. This place is massive."

Under the spellbreakers' scrutiny, fully mantled mages huddled in groups while young magi scurried by with tomes and parchments in their arms and packs overflowing with components. Higher up, a myriad of iron chandeliers hung, though Veen suspected the ample light had a magical helping hand.

Spotting EAST on a brass plaque, Veen guided his friends to the stairwell set inside the thick stone of the Tower's exterior wall.

As their steps echoed upward, Elanis grumbled, "I've visited four Towers in my short life, and each has had the rudest, most choleric arse greeting the public. One of these days I'm going to ask an archivist if they simply misunderstand the role of paralibrarian or if they purposely want the people to hate us."

Veen turned right down the hall on the third floor as instructed. Elanis put her arm out to stop him. With a cautious expression, she wandered toward the closed door of their potential new benefactor's quarters. "Strange . . ." Her face tensed. The door opened.

Taller than most members of the Hook mercenary guild, Nelis ducked under the doorframe as he exited the quarters in his long gambeson, tattered sleeves, and worn trousers. His right hand vised a bundle of scrolls. A split-second after Nelis's bald head turned their way, reprimand arched his eyebrow. He shut the door behind him deliberately. "Youse all show up late and without your leader? Making grand impressions, are we?"

Older than the rest of the band at twenty-seven years, Nelis tended to treat them all like pups. Veen hadn't missed that.

Nelis marched past them. Veen and Oren followed.

Elanis didn't budge. "We were detained. Shall we meet with Mage Curtiss?" The question was more of a command.

Nelis didn't break his stride. "If you want to try your luck, go on. I've got the missive, the map, and the Lekelithian blood a man like Dreanen trusts. But by all means, force him to explain it all again, yeah? Our benefactors love that. Doubly so for a Racinian."

"Dreanen?" Veen asked. Gruff as he could be, Nelis wasn't typically so informal with their benefactors.

Elanis cleared the fog from her spectacles with a kerchief before she finally gave in and joined Veen at the stairs. "Your brother is a massive shite."

"I've heard this somewhere before," Veen teased.

When the spellbreakers parted for their exit, Veen spied a violation beyond the river-reed thatch of New Market. Between the wealthiest estates in Aontus, scaffolding shielded an affront to the lowlanders: the new Temple of Rethfor. He scoffed. Rethfor knew where his true home was, with the lowlanders, not the coin worshippers.

He'd have asked his brother about their villagers' opinion of the new temple if Elanis hadn't continued her squabble with Nelis in the courtyard. Veen stood away from them with Oren and waited. The bickering carried on until Teague's lean form arrived. Tilting a grin on his vulpine face, he appeared unaffected by his da's shaming, and possibly downright cheery. Veen suspected he'd lost part of his argument with his father; his leathers had been given over for a dark blue version of the required attire of an elite male: breeches, hose, and an embroidered jerkin.

Nelis went straight to Teague and handed over the rolled parchment.

"Aye, thanks," their leader said. "We'll need to go somewhere private to talk this over, and I know just the place, so I do." Guiding them north along Pearl Street, he leaned close to Nelis and asked, "Is this a five-person job, or should I send for Joseb?"

Elanis cast a sidelong glance. "Teague, luck alone dictates all six of us—"

"Leave the duke to his frilly court and his dying king," Nelis interrupted. "We can manage a burglary without the sorcerer. Easy lift and go."

Veen shared a skeptical look with Elanis. The past three years had taught them Hook work was never that simple.

Chapter 2: Deviants' at Heart

Dread tightened Veen's chest when Teague halted the mercenaries in front of the Mercantile Guild hall, identified by five golden keys embedded high in the marble facade. On the veranda spanning the building's front, nosy nobles leered and lingered about the opened doors. Clothing consisted of breeches and hose, bell-shaped skirts and high-collared jerkins, mostly promoting the Racinian trend of ruby-red hues.

"You call this private?" Nelis asked.

"Aye," Teague answered. "We Fuchs have a nook in the ballroom. Private enough for my da's dealings, private enough to review our missive and swap tales of our recent adventures."

Risking her immunity to the patrons' scrutiny, Elanis placed her hand on Veen's shoulder and asked, "Teague, assuming we are still welcome at your father's estate, are you planning to jeopardize our shelter with this display?" Moneyed younglings emphasized her point by outright sneering

9

at Oren.

"Display?" Teague asked innocently. "I'm treating my friends to a nice fine meal, so I am. Besides, he'd never deny you shelter, my good mage. Your Tower is his best customer."

Veen snickered. "A rare day, indeed, to find Elanis and Nelis agreeing, no?"

"With the same face, too," Oren added.

Teague and Elanis glowered at the mirthful duo.

"Twice now."

Teague ignored the derision and strutted inside. Nelis shoved Veen after him. The band followed the privileged son past the steel of the guards' blades and into the foyer. Healthy wafts of steak wet Veen's tongue. They hadn't eaten since breakfast, but his mind didn't linger on his appetite long.

Stairs flared down to the proper entrance of the marbled hall. The whole room sang of pre-war alliances with Racine. White fleurs-de-lis had been stenciled on the mirrored walls, stitched into the servants' uniforms, and embossed on every silver candlestick, sconce, and chandelier in sight. Thankfully, there wasn't an oil painting of King Clyde hanging in sight; otherwise, Nelis would have torched the place at best—and the diners at worst.

Oren quietly asked Veen, "Did we not leave this country at dawn?"

For fear an echo could be heard over the loud exclamations of agreement, detestation, or boredom from the nobles below, Veen replied just as quietly, "'Tisn't my Lekelith down there." He brushed his hands through his hair.

Teague spread silence as he led the mage, the ax-toting Caperi, and the boggytrotters to a line of waiting servants. Only lilting notes fluttering from the room beyond challenged his voice. "We'll take our nook, if ye please."

A young woman with blonde curls kissing her freckled cheeks timidly stepped forward to say, "Of course, Master Fuchs." She looked to Oren. "Would you like to leave your pack in our care?"

If her aim had been to disarm Oren with her cheerful brown eyes, she failed. Accepting his decline, she sauntered ahead of them. Veen flinched when Nelis shoved him toward the ballroom.

The song was winding down when they entered. On a stage to their right, a frail bard refreshed her pipes while her companion tuned his lute. Nobles exited the dance floor to rejoin their drinks at the tables lining the tapestried walls, which placed their tutting disapproval directly in Veen's path. Some recognized Teague and began murmuring and hissing judgment, even outright pointing. Veen stuck close to his brother, who resembled a cat cornered by an excited child.

At the back of the room, a dark-paneled wall sported a row of hefty tapestries. Their escort went to a red-and-white weaving of a country setting and furled it back to reveal a deep nook with a high window of stained glass, a long mahogany table, and a dozen chairs. She bound the tapestry back with a white rope and promised Aled would see to them soon.

Veen watched her go. "I'll get us a round."

Setting the scrolls on the table, Teague pulled out a chair for Elanis and said, "Sit, Veen. They bring the drinks to us here."

Teague waited until Veen and Oren sat opposite them to take his seat between Elanis and Nelis. Bouncing a few times on the cushioned seat, Veen determined this was the one advantage he'd acknowledge this place had over any old-market tavern.

Nelis's mouth twisted in distaste for the foreign culture on Lekelith's soil. Luckily, the musician came to their rescue with a few strummed notes from his lute.

Ladies curtsied in a line across the parquet dance floor from bowing men. They moved forward to press their fingertips against their partners'. The bard joined with her song. Velvet bell-shaped skirts crumpled as the men spun the ladies too close together. For a moment, Veen stared, mesmerized by how joyful they appeared, downright playful when they weren't speaking.

Sinking back into his chair, Nelis crossed his arms. "So youse all survived Frysta Avfall?"

Oren scoffed in amusement. "You doubt our skills without you?"

Nelis made a playful face.

Oren's grin tightened with curiosity. "We could have used your muscles. Ogres do not fall easily."

Nelis bucked his shoulders once. "Sorry. Needed to be home is all."

"That's all?" Teague asked. "We dodged boulders and ran away from ogres for three weeks, and that is your explanation?"

Smiling wryly, Nelis said, "Ach, leave it a surprise, yeah?"

"Intriguing," Teague said.

"Whatever the surprise," Veen put in, "we're glad you're with us now, Brother." Fishing into his worn leather belt pouch, Veen picked out five bone dice and clattered them on the table. "How 'bout a game of specks?"

Elanis put her hand over the dice. "This doesn't strike me as the type of establishment where gambling is encouraged, Veen."

"Sure smells like the taverns that do," Veen said. He winked. "Smoke must've confused me."

Turning his attention from whatever Nelis had whispered, Teague said, "Nonsense. What's the point of using my father's status if we cannot enjoy ourselves?"

"The thing is . . ." Nelis said, eyeing the exit. He thumbed to Veen and back to himself. "Our kind doesn't belong here. We'd be in better company in an old-market tavern, yeah?" He stood.

"Ye lads are my company!" Teague said with the air of a command. "To anyone who has a problem with that . . ." He splayed two of his fingers and thrust them up for the room to see. Then he repeated the gesture with both hands. "Goes double for ol' Master Fuchs, father of a 'highborn mercenary and well-bred disappointment.'"

Veen chuckled uncomfortably, afraid to check if anyone had noticed outside the nook.

"Ambush me in the docks, does he?" Teague asked, folding his arms. "Suppose a big, grand display is best when you're shaming your son to still the neighbors' tongues. So let me play his game, lads."

"Sige," Oren said. "If it refills your pride, we will stay." Reaching his bare arm to his pack, Oren brought out a cloth, a vial of oil, and a whetstone. He unlashed one of his sacred axes and glided a thumb over the edge. Green and yellow paint interwove up the teak shaft to the carving of a crested songbird, identifying his clan back on the now deserted island of Caper.

The familiar sight of Oren sharpening his blades relaxed Nelis's shoulders. "All right, all right. Then let's leave our mark." He brought out his own blade and sat. The tip of Nelis's short sword jammed into the mahogany table. Magic ignited inside the blade, making it flare orange. A tendril of smoke escaped the supple wood as Nelis scored his name. Speechless, the band watched him then carve Teague's. The tan Teague had acquired in Frysta Avfall waned.

"A shame to scar such craftsmanship," Oren said, "no matter what you think of its owner."

Nelis asked, "'Runt' or 'Stille,' Runt?" He'd started carving "Runt" before Veen could answer. "What about you, Elanis? Should I put 'mage' for ya?"

Rising to work free the knot holding back the tapestry, Elanis said, "Leave me out of it, Nelis."

The tapestry fell, restoring some of their privacy behind its stitched carts hauling wool, barley, and peat. It couldn't quiet the unbridled laughter of wealthy men with drinks.

"Mage of Racine," Nelis said. "The smartest of all the magi."

Elanis glared at the vandal.

Nelis laughed. "I'm only teasin' ya."

"I won't tolerate any perceived slight from me creating trouble for Ameera's ascension."

"Oh." Nelis snorted. "The princess is still your true one, then?"

Teague put his hand up to pacify Elanis, but Oren killed the coming argument by saying, "A fool would deny such a powerful ally, even if only an ally in fair weather."

Predictably, Elanis replied, "She is my friend."

Veen sighed; it had been nice not to hear that argument for a few weeks.

"Fine. And Oren Ko." Finished, Nelis noticed Veen's apologetic wince at Teague. "What? 'Tisn't on fire, no?"

"No, Nelis," Elanis said. "You demonstrated great restraint. So much restraint, I wonder if you're crushing that bug up your arse."

The blade blazed, scorching the table black before Nelis lifted it. His eyes softened when Teague leaned between their challenging stares. The steel cooled to gray. Nelis put the weapon away and said to Veen, "Our da's rolling over in his grave. Us being in a place like this."

"The war is long over," Teague said.

"Perhaps not," Elanis remarked. "A crier in the docks said the Albacore sank after leaving Aontus. A Racinian galleon loaded with nobles makes a tempting target for Lekelithian supremacists."

"More importantly," Veen said, leaning forward, "prisoners escaped the Five Snakes? Never thought that'd happen. And what's this about missing lowlanders, Nelis?"

"No one we know, Runt. Teallaigh Te's fine. I was there this morning." His dismissal was too convincing. There was something he wasn't saying. Nelis cleared his throat. "Where are our drinks? I've an awful throat on me."

On cue, the tapestry flapped. Two attendants delivered loaves of warm buttered bread; plates of splayed roasted apple slices, sugared strawberries, and carmine olives; and a pewter pitcher of wine. Veen helped himself to a strawberry, wiping the excess sticky sugar on his tunic.

"Master Fuchs," a lanky servant said in his singsong Patevian accent.

He slid the olives within Teague's reach. "Pleasure it is to have you here, sir. I am Aled. Is there anything else you and your company desire?"

"Stout," Nelis said. "Five. The darker the better. And oysters."

"Oysters?" Aled asked, playfully offended. He spied Nelis's carving. His mouth dropped open until he stammered, "We do serve the freshest scallops in Lekelith. Piquant tarts. Bay prawns. Glazed chops. Mille-feuille. Profiteroles."

Elanis's eyes lit up, but Nelis repeated, "Oy-sters."

Oren raised his fingers to stall Aled's quick departure. "Do you have rum?"

As Elanis altered her ale and oysters to a cream tea, Nelis tore a hunk of bread free and devoured his snack while Veen sampled the olives.

When the tapestry fell back in place behind the attendants, Teague nodded. "On a fairy's wings, word will reach my father within the hour."

Elanis huffed.

Oren said, "We never agreed; why does the Hook want a half-ogre brute?"

"A half-ogre?" Nelis asked. "That's why youse were sent to Frysta Avfall?"

Veen nodded and added, "We decided against strength. Joseb's right; we've enough muscle-brained mercs."

The insult accompanying that suggestion from Joseb translated for Nelis without exact wording. Nelis grimaced but asked, "Who else went?"

"A recruit took your place," Elanis said. "Remy. A pik." Surprisingly, Nelis grinned when the others laughed.

"A wee tiny one, too," Veen put in. "Only as high as my waist."

"I amn't bothered," Nelis said. "A fellow lowlander?"

"Nay," Teague answered, sliding the olives closer to Veen and pulling the strawberries to himself. "A Racinian."

"Anyroads," Nelis gruffed, "'tis a good thing I stayed; someone arrived on time to get our next assignment."

Veen received a weary glance from Elanis.

That killed Teague's mirth, too. "Ah, yes. Work." He worked at the knots binding the forgotten scrolls. But the partition curled back again, interrupting their privacy with the powerful scent of the sea.

A silver platter was lowered before Nelis, stacked high enough with half-shelled oysters the serving could near-well have fed their entire village. Though many lowlanders in Teallaigh Te were piks.

"To your earlier question, Nelis," Teague said, receiving his ale from Aled. "Aye, we found a half-ogre and delivered him for the trials. Let's hope we don't get sent back to Frysta Avfall anytime soon. I've had my fill of numb toes and frozen noses." He smirked at Nelis. "And the barbarians are not generous lovers."

Bug-eyed, Aled lifted his hand to his heart.

Veen swiped another cold olive and chuckled as he sucked the salty flesh from around the pit. He spit the seed on the floor, to Aled's further dismay. Sitting up straight, Veen said, "Imagine. That brute has to test in feckin' Trône d'Argent. The Racinians'll be pissin' themselves when they see that giant coming down the street. With Joseb. And Remy." He nearly forgot his company before adding, "No offense," for Elanis's sake.

Smiles all around, except Nelis and Aled. "Better him than me," Nelis murmured. "Thank Rethfor, the trials were in Patevia when you finally hit seventeen, Runt." His brother winked for their secret. What's one year, give or take, when you need to eat?

Oren set aside his sharpening and reached for an oyster. He raised his drink. "To three years, my friends. Mabuhay!" The others lifted half-shells and their pewter mug or porcelain cup, clacking them all together. They tossed back the oysters, then drank. Elanis stole a pull from Veen's ale while her tea cooled.

When the servants had gone, Teague shoved the platters aside and unfurled the scrolls on the table.

Nelis sucked down another oyster. "Like I said, 'tis a pinch job. We're to be silent and speedy. Ghosts in the night."

"What are we stealing?" Teague asked. "Gold?"

Nelis shook his head. "One chest." He flattened a small cut of parchment that bore a detailed drawing. Five roses decorated the lid of a bejeweled chest.

Teague passed the drawing over to Elanis and studied a map. "The Boyd Estate?"

Nelis shrugged.

"Why does Mage Curtiss want it?" Veen asked.

His brother's first answer came in the form of a sharp-eyed shut-the-feck-up. "He didn't say."

"What's in it?" Elanis asked. The question went unanswered until Teague glowered at Nelis.

"Don't know. Didn't ask."

Teague said, "You're supposed to ask these things, Nelis. Keeps the Hook from becoming venal riffraff, so it does."

Elanis set aside the drawing. "When we were in the Tower, I felt something . . ." She sighed. "I don't know what it was, which is what worries me. There was an unfamiliar tingle coming from Mage Curtiss's quarters."

"Unfamiliar?" Nelis asked. "Now you're an expert in all magics?"

"I've been inside the Tower of Trône d'Argent's vaults, Nelis van Veen! I know a thing or two about rare magics, and can assure you the rarer they are, the more risk is involved." She tapped her fingertips on the table. "But it was gone so quickly . . . Perhaps I'm mistaken."

Shaking his head, Nelis said, "He's a Lekelithian mage, not a Merithian speaker. Besides, Clarkson already told him we'd do it, didn't he?"

Teague winced out a soft agreement. It was still Teague's right to decide, no matter what their guild master's initial reply had been.

Nelis continued, "Dreanen says we scout the estate for three nights starting tomorrow. Then we make our move. When we do, we're to bring it directly to him in the Wives' prayer room of the new temple. He'll open the lock."

"Three nights?" Veen asked. "That's a wee much."

"Definitely maybe," Teague answered. "'Tisn't a royal vault." Worry crinkled the corners of his small eyes. "I don't care for this, lads." They sat in silence, waiting for Teague to deny the job outright. It had happened twice before.

Nelis looked Teague in the eye. "All I know is, the lowlanders need this. That's the one thing Dreanen was clear about."

"But not how they'd benefit," Teague replied, letting Elanis study the map.

"Perhaps it's connected to the missing lowlanders?" she asked. "At least then I'd understand your willingness to trust this mage."

Oren swirled the rum concoction in his goblet. "That should be our focus. If your people are vanishing, we can spare a week and the coin of one job to find them."

Holding up a hand, Nelis hedged, "After this, then, yeah? As far as we really know, those are just rumors."

Veen frowned.

"This feels more important, Runt."

"Yes," Elanis said. "There are two lowlanders here. What do you think, Veen?"

Veen's gut froze. He thought and answered, "If both aid the lowlanders, shouldn't we commit to the one we know—we suspect is true? More true. More reliable?"

Nelis gave a satisfied nod.

Veen inhaled.

Elanis gave away nothing in her unblinking expression. She sipped her tea before saying, "Veen has offered to have us visit your Teallaigh Te tomorrow so we may experience a true immersion into your folksy parlance. We shall inspect these rumors while you attend to your superfluous spying."

"Can't," Nelis said sharply. "Not Oren. I need help counting the weasels and whistles at the estate. 'Tisn't a cottage we're scouting, yeah?"

A sigh was Oren's only response. The Caperi put his ax away and drew out its twin to resume his scraping.

"Sad and true," Teague said with a tolerant expression for Nelis. "I won't be able to help the lads, not when my mother knows I'm about town. But no reason El and Veen cannot investigate on their own. Be mindful, yes?"

Finishing her scone with a large bite, Elanis laid the map before Oren. She swallowed the rest of her tea without taking a breath. "Well, then," she said rising. "The evening is about to begin, gentlemen. Nelis. And I am determined to enjoy myself; that is, if we have finished nurturing your grudge."

Teague gave in with a nod.

"Come, Veen. Be my little brother for the evening and show me the sights of this Aontus."

As he rose, Veen asked Nelis, "You're staying at Teague's with us, yeah?"

His brother shook his head.

"You should," Teague said. "I may need a seasoned warrior to fight my way into my own chambers." Nelis opened his mouth to disagree, but Teague cut him off. "Don't make me order you."

The merchant's son tapped two fingers to his brow for Elanis and Veen. "Ta, ye two. Have your fun. The guards will expect ye. My tower is down the passage to the left."

"Your tower?" Nelis asked with slight panic.

"Aye, I'm well-to-do and handsome," Teague replied, sweeping his hand toward the dance floor. "Care for a dance to assess your chances? I'll let you lead."

Nelis tensed at the jest.

Elanis wrapped her arm around Veen's. Component pouches created lumps beneath her draping sleeve, the very reason mages always smelled like florists and spice merchants. "You needn't wait up," she said.

"Runt!" Nelis called, bringing heat to Veen's cheeks. "You wearing your necklace?"

Veen groaned. "Always."

After a satisfied nod from Nelis, Elanis briskly dragged Veen across the dance floor before the dainty songbird could start up again. Judged by the assembly as he traveled from the nook to the door, he didn't fully breathe until he was out of the fermented fug and the damp air refreshed his face. His breath fogged in the lamplight holding back the thickening darkness.

Flipping his hood up, he casually walked backward. "What'd you like to see? A tavern where the buxom petals gather?"

Elanis donned the silver hood of her mantle. "Why not?" Her heels clacked against the bricks as they strolled through New Market. "And they had better be pretty."

With a long exhale, she stopped. "No. Carousing can wait. I think first the Tower of Aontus deserves a second chance. Then, after full dark and exactly one sherry in a tavern obnoxiously loud with reed flutes and the aforementioned cleavage, my dear obedient little brother, we should take an extemporaneous tour of the vault in the Boyd Estate."

"Oh, aye." He laughed it off and set their path to fulfill her first request. And yet his mind recited her jest while she shopped in the Tower's Emporium, considered it again while she coaxed the new paralibrarian on shift into allowing them a glimpse of the libraries, and thought on it a third time while she retrieved her fourth sherry at the tavern just inside the old market.

Amid the reek of dockworkers and weak ale, Veen felt at home. At least, his home on the mercenary road. All it needed was a little mischief.

Six bouncing women trounced the stage arm in arm as the fiddler set their rhythm. Taking her eyes from the true draw of the tavern, Elanis squinted at him. "What?"

Raising one shoulder, he asked, "What if we did crack the nut?"

"Steal the chest?" She scoffed and rolled her eyes.

Veen sat forward and delivered a playful grin. "Teague did want answers."

Elanis glanced at him again, then turned to face him fully. "He's more prone to lock us both away for our own protection than to thank us. Oren and Nelis would stand guard."

"Just repeating your idea," Veen teased.

Leaching courage from her and giving the best he could muster in return, he smirked. By the time her lips curled, the notion had grown into a stupidly inspirational necessity, a once-in-a-lifetime opportunity to claim youth or decline it outright. The bargaining ended with fairy grins in their eyes.

"Very well," Elanis said, raising her glass. "Let's crack the nut." They emptied their drinks and strode out of the tavern taller than before.

Chapter 3: Cracking the Nut

Veen stood watch in the woods hiding behind the Boyd Estate's fifteen-foot wall of mortared stone as Elanis flipped her mantle over to the dull black underside. She crouched and began assembling a spell. Her palm-sized brass medallion of a peacock emitted a faint blue glow and dropped onto the leaves.

"That bastard at the Tower's Emporium had to have been lying," she said. Her fingers worked to weave the stems of several plants into a small wreath. "What kind of nursery doesn't have heliotrope? I'd wager every one of their mages grows some in the arboretum 'for study.'"

"You didn't mind when we were there."

"I thought I would have time to find some." She let her hands fall to her lap in defeat. Her mouth opened, threatening to end the thrilling whim that had brought them there, and closed. "The problem is I only have enough to hide myself. I can render you invisible without the heliotrope, but the spell will dissipate the first time you break wind." Veen snickered as she continued. "Or cough or sneeze or swallow too hard or take a heavy step."

"Three ales in," Veen said, "I can't make you any promises."

Elanis grinned.

"Better work together, yeah?"

She slipped the wreath into one of her linen pouches, tied it, and tucked it into place up her left sleeve. "Of course." After hiding the component pouches and her peacock up her right sleeve, she rose and gestured in the direction of the garden gate, another hundred feet away from the estate's private road. "I'm ten for ten, prepared either way."

Veen loosed a small laugh and led the way under the leaves whispering in the fresh air. "Eight of those spells will alert the guards. If we're discovered, we'll wish you had those pouches for Nelis."

"Nonsense," she said. "There's enough rowan, heather, and cabbage in Lekelith to create a mélange suitable for him." Her shoulders bucked as she giggled.

The jest eluded Veen, but he grinned politely.

One guard and his halberd protected the hedge-framed garden gate. Elanis entered a clearing as the clouds broke above. Her red skirt caught the moonlight like a bucket of oil catching fire. Veen jerked her back into the shadows.

"Back the other way?" he whispered.

"What? Why? It's one guard."

His thumbs fondled the handles of his daggers. "Those wild fairies in your head will send you to Merith next if you keep listening to them."

She hummed her agreement. "Certainly before Nelis." Her hand removed a pouch from her left sleeve. "Not to worry; Sir Guard of the Garden won't remember a thing." She paused. "I do wish we'd found more heliotrope. For the derring-do I've mustered, I'd prefer not to leave you at greater risk to the consequences of failure."

His toothy grin vanquished their final path out. "Don't worry about me. Your fashion's what needs hiding, Racinian."

"Oh!" Elanis gasped in false offense before slapping his shoulder. "Master van Veen, you've cut me to the bone." She sneered down at herself. "Seriously, don't remind me. I feel like I'm smuggling dwarves under this overwrought skirt. One on each hip."

Elanis untied the pouch, brought it to her nose, and winced. "Gods, that's awful." Scanning their surroundings, she whispered, "Hold your breath." She readied her throw. "Profund somni." A vapor erupted from the mouth of the pouch before she flung it straight into the hedge framing the gate. Golden dust exploded to envelope the hedge. Metal clanked against the pathway's tiles. When the glittery cloud dissipated, the guard lay unconscious.

Waving away the remnants lingering in the air, Elanis yawned. "Come," she said, rushing the gate. "That particular spell expunges memories of the past few moments. He'll believe he dozed off and shall wake in a few hours with a headache that'll do any morning regret proud."

Stepping over the soldier, Veen swung the wooden gate into something. He shoved the obstacle aside, scraping metal across the tiled path. "Both of them?" he asked. The second guard snoozed as soundly as the first.

"Two guards? Well, that was lucky."

Veen drew his daggers and dashed past the beds spilling their branches into the path. From the squat shadow of a central fountain, he surveyed the hedge-walled courtyard. If Veen had to guess, he's say the chaos of the garden belonged to a Racinian who droned on about textures and fragrance clusters. Flowers tall and wide, grasses sharp and short all mingled in wild abandon.

Elanis's hand searched inside the hedge. Once she had retrieved her pouch, she rushed to duck next to Veen on the tiles.

Dark windows dotted the pale stone of the four-story manor above the hedges. A balustrade along its roof suggested ramparts for more guards. "How do people live like this?" he asked.

"Full of pride, I'd imagine," Elanis answered. She smirked. "Speaking of, if discretion is what we're after, a devious thought has occurred to me, one guaranteeing the guards never mention their slumber."

His smirk grew to match hers. "Maybe just to be safe, yeah?"

After setting the undressed guards into a comfy snuggle among the tulips, they chuckled their way into the last section of the gardens.

No sooner had they dipped behind a cold iron bench than two guards appeared at the hedged exit. Twice luck had saved their rumps, and they hadn't even made it into the manor. The shiny blades of the halberds swayed when the guards finally left.

Veen sprinted to the hedges and spied out to the sprawling lawn, which provided an unobstructed view of the new Temple of Rethfor. He squeezed his daggers. The Aontus nobles had built the temple in a valley beneath them!

Studying the manor, he spotted a servants' door fifty feet away. No guards on the ramparts. His fingers beckoned Elanis.

"Veen, look." She snapped off a sprig and joined him. "Lavender for luck. A reminder the wealthy are just as superstitious as the rest of us humans."

He sniffed. "Their servants are." She conceded with a sigh, and stowed the twig behind her belt. "Time to disappear, El."

"You're sure you wouldn't prefer to be the invisible one?"

"Get on with you! Remember the way?"

Her weary head tilt recited her argument; if she'd seen it, she remembered it. Untying the pouch with the wreath inside, Elanis tilted it toward her spectacles and whispered, "Odobrat'z dohl'adu." She vanished.

Two taps on his shoulder told him to move. "Right," Veen breathed. "Gods keep us from harm." After rechecking the ramparts, the lawn, and the windows, he scampered for the round-topped servants' entrance. Unlocked, thank Rethfor. The faint smell of meat pies welcomed him to a dark hallway. Veen held the door ajar until he felt a tug on his wrist.

Led through the empty corridor to the kitchen, Veen let his eyes adjust to the darkness that was barely lessened by a dying fire in the oven. A long preparation table divided the kitchen. Suddenly certain Nelis would lash his bum as red as the apples piled high on the table, Veen struggled to hear over his heartbeat.

Elanis led him down to the table and into a hallway at the base of the servants' stairway. She released him. He froze. Abruptly, her hand smashed his face, pressing him back into the kitchen. Two voices approached. On the scrap-covered floor, Veen squeezed himself under the preparation table and fought to slow his breathing.

Three men entered with a light flickering off their polished boots. They trod the crumbs to the far end of the room. A bottle was uncorked. "Let them," a husky voice said. "'Twon't be long before it belongs to us again. The king will steer us straight."

The king? King Clyde? Joseb had said the man was on his deathbed.

Next to Veen's ear, a mouse chewed on a dried shred of blackened meat. The bold little fecker didn't even flinch when Veen jerked away from it.

"Our schedule is tight," a Racinian said. "Aside from that, we've little reason to worry."

Suddenly, the mouse raced for the gap under the larder door. Elanis's invisible hands maneuvered Veen's arms up over his head. A quick tug on his forearms started him slowly slipping out the far end of the table and into the hall as the men continued their discussion.

"There had better not be," the husky voice said.

Now moving across the floorboards in the hall, Veen grinned at the thought of a servant walking in on the sight of him sliding along by sheer force of will. At least he did until Elanis thumped his cheek.

At the servants' stairs, she helped him upright. He gingerly followed up the creaky steps. A wad of his tunic jerked away from his chest. Elanis hauled him along faster. If patience was the key ingredient to this pie, she'd lost her appetite.

On the third floor, the door swung wide. Light poured in from the residence. Elanis's prodding prompted him onto the plush red carpets and into the distinct essence of old parchment in the air.

A spiraling stairway led down to a grand library. However, Elanis pulled him straight along a walkway shielded from view by only a low railing. Veen skirted the wall. Candlelight reflected off the ancient Merithian plates and shields decorating every nook and cranny of their path.

Veen dared a glance down to the shelved tomes and polished tables. An elder noble mulled over a map at an ebony desk. He held the map close to a candle's flame. Veen squinted to see what had enthralled the man, but Elanis jerked him onward.

Their trek ended inside a private library with shelves laden with golden weapons and age-old curiosities. "Ach, blasted discretion," Veen mumbled. "'Tisn't too much to ask that we pocket a trinket—for a memento, yeah?"

The window unlatched and swung out toward the tapping rain. Elanis reappeared before it with a patronizing expression for his question. "This is our exit."

Veen nodded.

She knuckled her back. "Thank your gods you don't weigh more than seven stone."

Moving behind a formidable writing desk flanked by two white-and-red vases, Elanis whisked aside a tapestry of some battle or another to reveal an iron panel from floor to ceiling. "The map was correct," she said. "The vault lies beyond this. That and the Merithian decor lend credence to Mage Curtiss's claims. There'll be no sleep lost due to stealing from this lot."

"I could have told you that outside, so."

Absorbed by the puzzle set waist-high in the iron panel, Elanis tapped one of the twelve brass knobs. Her breath fogged one as she knelt before them. "I don't sense any wards." Shooing him back, she said, "You're in my light. Go keep watch while I work through this."

Veen crept out to the railing over the larger library. The three men from the kitchen had returned with drinks in hand. Dressed for the Racinian court, they were younger than Veen had imagined.

"Harold," the old noble at the desk said to the Racinian, "take a look." He held out the map.

Ducking below the rail, Veen listened.

"No," Harold said in awe. "You've found it?"

"Not more than a day outside of Trône d'Argent," the old man replied. "I tell you, a cache worth the blood." Veen peeked over the rail but couldn't see the map. "Cheers to the king, lads!" Glass clinked. "We'll have more to celebrate in a few days than we had anticipated."

"Then my bed calls to me," Harold said. "I now have a voyage to Trône d'Argent at dawn."

Veen crawled away to check on Elanis's progress. Frozen in thought, Elanis stood before the ajar panel.

"How'd you do that?" he asked.

"Fat, greasy fingers," she answered. "Brass was a terrible choice on their part. But Veen . . ." White as a ghost, she stared into the dark vault. It was too dark for his eyes. He nudged her. "Yes, of course." As she reached up her left sleeve, she bit her lip. "Shut the door," she said without inflection. Worse than he'd estimated, she'd already gone into the void she sought when fearing her own emotions.

"What's spooked ya?"

As he did her bidding, she tossed a pouch into the vault and whispered, "Fywiogi at graidd." Like fireflies in summer, specks of light drifted from the pouch to cling to the walls. The vault glowed as though the moon shone directly inside.

Veen ambled in to study the room. Seven gray cloaks hung on the far wall. Identical gray masks bearing a long nose and narrow eyes shared their pegs. Aside from the gilded chest in a recess on his left, the room wasn't much of a treasury.

From the doorway, Elanis pointed timidly at the far wall. "Something vile hides behind the shortest cloak."

Veen passed through the spell's lingering rosemary scent. Carefully brushing one of the youth-sized cloaks aside, he found another peg suspending a cracked leather collar. "A speaker's collar?" A magus-enslaver. Even with no magic for the collar to steal, he hesitated to touch it. "How do we destroy it?"

"Melt the token in its center," Elanis answered matter-of-factly.

Veen slipped the collar behind his belt. "As soon as we can, yeah?"

Elanis's fingers fidgeted as she thought. Veen went to her and took her hands in his. "How did something like that survive the Revolt of the Magi, Veen?" she asked. "Who are these people?"

He kept his suspicions about Racine's involvement in their plot to himself. "C'mon now. We're still free to have our fun, El." She nodded, slowly coming back to him. Veen leaned back and eyed the chest in the recess. "There she is."

Elanis entered the vault fully to see for herself. Pink enameled roses, jade, and diamonds provided most of the chest's sparkle. The golden lines on its white surface reminded Veen of the quilt his ma had left him.

"Must be worth a fortune!" Veen said. They both ran a hand over the design encrusting the lid in a gemstone bouquet of roses.

"If I'm honest," Elanis said, "I'm afraid to discover what else the Boyds would lock away."

"We could strike off now if you want."

"Perish the thought." Elanis bent to examine the lock. "Did Mage Curtiss expect us to carry this beast back to him?"

"Aye. Oren and Nelis could." Veen scratched his chin. "We could pry it."

"Too obvious. See if you can pick it."

He reached into his pocket for the lockpicks Nelis had given him at Winter Peak. "You know yourself I'm not any good at this."

Standing over him, she crossed her arms over her chest. Big sister, indeed.

"Joseb could have opened it," he remarked, aware of how any admiration of sorcery put Elanis's hackles up.

"And then blow you to pieces with a passing irritation." She retrieved her pouch and returned to his side as he worked.

Veen fiddled with his best fiddling effort. But the picks didn't seem to connect with the pins no matter the angle. A good fifteen minutes of scratching the inside of the lock and Veen dripped like ice in a sunbeam. He growled, "No. 'Tis not feckin' working!"

"Very well," Elanis said. "Go stand in the corner and look away."

"What?"

"Do it."

Veen moved to stand by the cloaks. The gray masks watching him forced his eyes elsewhere. He glanced back.

Elanis waved her fingers at the lock, then clenched them. A clunk sounded. The lid popped up. Her eyes met his. "Never. Speak. Of this. To anyone."

He knelt next to her. "How proud Joseb would be—"

"Never!"

When Veen agreed, she raised the lid. Inside, a black satin pillow held an oblong white stone as large as a shoe. Chills darted through Veen's limbs as memories of his parents overpowered his senses. He fell back and scrambled to his feet.

"What?" Elanis asked. Veen's eyes bulged when her hands lifted the stone from its perch. Pink tinged the stone around her touch.

"The—the Heart of Rethfor."

"The lowlanders' stone?" she asked. "Amazing. It truly is warm, almost hot." She pressed it into his arms. "A god's relic? In the same room as a speaker's collar?"

The Heart warmed his bones as soon as it met his skin. Years of memories before the revolution, before it had been just he and Nelis, played out as best he remembered them. The happiest days of his life.

"Veen!" Elanis said, snapping him back to her.

"We can't leave it, El!" he said over whatever she was saying. "What's it doing here? 'Tis supposed to be in the temple in Teallaigh Te. Who'd steal it?"

Elanis smothered his words with her hand. "Hush!" She shut the jeweled chest. "Don't worry. We're not leaving behind a god's relic in the hopes it'll stay put."

He clutched the Heart to his chest. Pink swelled through the stone. "We've got to get out of here!"

They returned to the small library. Elanis dragged the high-backed chair from the desk to the window. A chill wind beat a path around the room as rain pelted the windowsill. She leaned outside. "I don't see the guards yet." After looking down, she stood away from the rain. "I'm having second thoughts about this route."

Replacing the tapestry over the sealed vault, Veen asked, "What spells do you have?"

"None that have empirically gone without notice, aside from a pigeon burst I always have handy for Nelis."

Veen exhaled loudly. "Quietly out the window or loudly through the manor, I don't care! Choose one now!"

Hiking up her skirt, Elanis climbed onto the chair and up to the inside sill. She balked at a wet gust and grimaced down at him.

Veen set the chair back at the writing desk. "Push the window closed when we step off."

Elanis whined as she searched the ground again.

He popped the medallion of his necklace into his mouth and hopped his buttocks up onto the sill. They shuffled into position on the outside ledge.

"Do you see the guards?" she asked hopefully.

He grunted and jerked his head toward the emptiness next to them. "Go you into your void."

Her eyebrows rose at his rudeness, but it appeared to work. Blocking her view of the fifty-foot drop as best he could, Veen wrapped his arms around her and clutched the Heart to her back. She buried her nails into him. "Step with me now," Veen said to her chest.

After a deep breath, he slowly blew across the taste of nickel on his tongue. As the air passed the medallion, his feet began to tingle. He pulled her from the ledge. Elanis shut the window as they hovered for a moment. Easing his blow, they floated down as gently as a fairy's sigh. The effect would last only as long as he had breath, so he kept his exhale steady and calm.

When the toes of his boots hit the grass, his lungs relished the inhale. Elanis resumed breathing herself.

They swaddled the Heart in Elanis's mantle and ran without stopping, past the cuddling guards, straight out to the private road leading back to New Market.

A few haunting notes from an all-too-familiar instrument sped Veen's steps. But Elanis's panting stopped. Arming his tongue with lies, Veen turned to face their failure. Oren approached from the woods and filled the distance with a few low notes from his small oblong hun. "I play a tune of mischief, and who do I summon?"

"You tracking us?" Veen asked.

"We were taking a quick look at the estate," Elanis answered, almost convincingly so. "Seems safe enough." She stretched and addressed Veen. "Oh, I can only guess the hour. We should get to bed." She walked on.

Oren called after her. "Teague's father has sent our things to the Marquis's Chaperone inn." His fingers tapped the clay instrument in his hands. "I know a thing or two about sacred objects, Veen. What has El let you wrap in hers?"

Chapter 4: Heart and Home

Nestled in a blanket before the fire in Elanis's excessively shiny and plush room at the Marquis's Chaperone, Veen handed Rethfor's Heart to Oren. Oren drew his hand across the white stone, leaving trails of pink that soon disappeared. As Veen relayed the events of their evening, Oren sopped up the tale better than bread in cream.

Then he soured. "You did this to anger Nelis."

Elanis ended her pacing. "Nonsense. We completed the investigation he neglected." She received her mantle from Veen and laid it flat on her bed. "What I can't decide is whether it's best to deliver the empty chest to Mage Curtiss or to tell Teague and Nelis what we've discovered."

"Or both," Veen added. He prayed for Rethfor to guide him, even if it meant Nelis would tan his hide.

Oren nodded. "Oo nga. If this Heart is sacred to your people, they will agree to deceive the mage."

"No," Elanis murmured. "I don't know. Nelis believes our benefactor has the lowlanders' best interests at heart. Excuse the pun." Her face grew concerned as she studied the stone from afar. "With a cult in the mix, I'm not willing to take the gamble just yet."

"Cult?" Oren asked.

"Secret society?" Elanis thought aloud. "Or maybe 'cult' is correct."

"Well," Veen hemmed, "we saw some men planning something." He didn't believe they were a cult as much as henchmen in King Clyde's pocket. "And they did have this." He removed the speaker's collar from his belt.

"Filii Cinere," Elanis said. "That was written on the panel sealing the vault." She sighed at their failed attempts to repeat the name. "Children of the Ashes. There were robes and masks with a Merithian nose in the vault." She gestured to the speaker's collar. "And that. I've never heard of the Filii Cinere, and Ameera would have mentioned a secret society if it touched the Racinian court."

"If she knew," Oren added. The Caperi's demeanor darkened. He snatched the speaker's collar from Veen. "Perhaps Nelis's plan was wiser than you thought?"

Elanis's eyes kept returning to the Heart with more fidgeting accompanying each glance.

"Speak your mind, El," Veen said.

She sighed and shook her head. "I was tired of wearing this monstrosity before it carried a pond in its folds. Leave me to bathe and prepare for our journey to Teallaigh Te. We'll decide what to do after we've rested. After being marched from Frysta Avfall to Ameera's court and onward to Aontus, I doubt one of us has the clarity to proceed right now." Her eyes never left the stone, suggesting she fully meant herself.

Veen's toes dug into the thick carpets as he stood and wrapped the Heart in his blanket. "At dawn, yeah?"

Elanis nodded.

"Got a couple of hours to sleep then."

"My suggestion," Oren said, "take El's lead and bathe. It was no mystery how those ogres found us."

Scowling, Veen shoved him. "Ach! Don't be like that, boy. I'm not that ripe!"

Elanis didn't refute it. "As I said, we'll have clearer minds—and more tact—once we've rested."

Oren laughed.

She pulled on the dangling strip of tapestry by the bed to sound the servants' bell downstairs.

Veen reached for the collar, but Oren held it above his reach. "If I decide to tell them," Oren said, narrowing his eyes, "this is my proof. They may not believe you two were so reckless."

"Yes, they would," Elanis muttered. "But, Oren—"

"I will melt it myself. I give my word." A knock on the door prompted Oren to hide the magus-enslaver inside his leaf-beetle vest.

A lanky man in a black tunic and hose greeted them with a slight bow. "Lady—em, Mage Kimball, how may I assist you at this hour?"

After Elanis requested her bath, Veen and Oren followed the porter into the hall. "A bath in our room, too," Oren said to the servant. "My friend stinks of fear and bad decisions."

Veen grumbled, "All right, all right."

Inside their room, Veen hid the Heart under a pillow before Oren collapsed on the downy mattresses. Three men arrived carrying a copper bathtub and set it in front of the fireplace. By the time they had finished filling it with buckets of steaming water, Oren was snoring soundly.

Stripped and freezing, Veen settled into the soapy warmth quickly. He almost forgave Oren a little. As he scrubbed, he asked, "Oren, you awake?" The snoring didn't stop. Veen raised his voice. "Oren, tell me about that undead dragon on your island."

One eye opened enough for Veen to see the shine of it. Oren groaned into his pillow. "Foul little man, I do not want to dream of Bus'baem tonight."

"I'm awake, fulfilling your request, amn't I? Least you could do is keep me company."

Emitting a low growl, Oren stretched and rose on his elbows. "Your brother will pay for making me bunk with you."

Not that he minded Nelis doing one of his disappearing-in-the-middle-of-the-night tricks tonight, but a passing concern for the abductions made Veen ask, "Where is himself?"

"Safe." Oren interrupted Veen's next question. "Do you expect us to scout the Boyd Estate after you two kicked the hornets' nest?" Judgment glared at Veen, churning his gut again.

"Whatever you say about it, say nothing, Oren."

"I do not care for secrets of this kind, Veen."

"I know, boy. I do. But you're the sensible kind. You'll side with us in the morning."

Satisfied with his scrubbing, Veen left the cooling water and toweled off. "Anyroads, we'll figure out what to do—El will—while we're in Teallaigh Te. But don't let Nelis get caught if the Boyds find we've taken it ahead of schedule, yeah?"

"Has Nelis wronged you?"

"You know he hasn't."

"Then you should trust him."

Sitting with his back to Oren, Veen retrieved the Heart from beneath the pillow and petted it. "Oren, this is grave serious. My gut says Nelis is better off never knowing the Heart was involved."

Oren eyed him expectantly.

But Veen shook his head. "Trust me. We'll brew up a grand plan in Teallaigh Te. Leave it until we're back. I'm pleading here, boy."

The sky through the window had lightened enough to tell Veen he'd be better off not to bother with sleep. The sooner he and Elanis were away, the better.

Oren didn't say anything while Veen dressed in his least filthy clothes. No need for leathers in Teallaigh Te. They'd serve better by protecting the Heart in his burlap bag. "You know where to find us."

"May the faeries leave your journey be," Oren said.

Veen laughed at the Lekelith farewell until a guilt-laden glance scolded him. "Too right."

Up a level, Veen knocked on Elanis's door. She answered in a similar state to his, all puffy-eyed, though thankfully back in trousers and high leather boots. Contrary to her griping over Racinian fashion, red thread created ruby patterns in the embroidery of her black jerkin and the hems of her bell sleeves.

"I saw our carriage arrive through the window," she said, retreating into her room. "You smell nice."

"I smell like Teague."

A servant arrived behind Veen.

Elanis donned her mantle and buttoned it before collecting her things with the servant's help. Veen declined assistance with his bag.

The stars were barely visible when Veen and Elanis reached the carriage at the front of the estate. With her possessions stowed, they relaxed against the padded seats for the four-hour journey through the countryside.

Buildings shrank and colors brightened as they trundled away from the city into full morning. More rapidly, the river-reed thatch turned to barley. City stink gave way to hay and honeysuckle with the crisp, dewy dawn taking over smooth, curving pastures where ancient chestnut trees lent their fat branches to weary lowlander travelers who didn't trust the city at night.

Teallaigh Te would take a few hours yet to reach; Veen stretched his legs and promised himself a nap.

Just as he was dozing off, Elanis asked, "Do they still have a problem with basilisks on this island?"

Veen didn't open his eyes. "Out west, in the crannogs, aye. Not this close to Aontus."

What felt like mere minutes passed before a coo from Elanis woke him. Her spectacles nearly blinded him with the reflected light of the sun. Sitting up, he caught sight of Mount Noafa through the window. The wheels of the carriage met the wooden bridge crossing the River Eagna's determined waters. They'd reached his village.

High atop Mount Noafa, weathered stone still bore the streaks of black from the night of his parents' deaths in Rethfor's true temple. "You see the braziers around the entry?" he asked, scooting closer. "The Wives of Rethfor keep them lit as a sign: sanctuary for all. 'With welcome, rest here in my warmth, my people of the lowlands.'" He wondered how the Wives felt about moving Rethfor's waiting home to Aontus.

Elanis wrinkled her brow. "I never pegged you as the devout sort."

"Just quiet about it." Veen kept her focused on the temple as they traveled to the village center, past the statues of his parents, and on to the most formidable building in Teallaigh Te, its sole inn and tavern, The Wayward Tulip. Judging by the wood-and-leather boggytrotter boots, most sized to fit little pik feet, and the peat-cutting tools lined against the brown rock facade, they were just in time for the midday crowd. That was unlucky.

Elanis climbed out behind him and read the sign engraved with tulips around a windmill. "The Wayward Tulip? Is that a euphemism?"

Veen considered it. "I never thought of that." He thinned his lips at her. "Do try to leave some of my childhood untarnished, will ya?"

Taking one of her bags with his free arm, he signaled for the driver to strike off.

She asked, "Did you not want a ride home?"

He scoffed. "Can't just leave you to face the locals alone, so."

Her right hand tugged on her mantle. "Surely I'll be fine."

Veen clicked his tongue at the comment and carried her bag forward. Without Nelis ducking the ceiling beams, Veen's entrance through the propped doors didn't draw attention. At most tables, dudeens tottered between the male patrons' lips, when not tapping their chins, and perfumed the air with pipe smoke sweeter than the smoke in the Mercantile Guild hall. A few of the pik wives played cards while their husbands gossiped.

The Tulip's familiarity eased the knots in his back. He strutted straight to the far side of the tavern's U-shaped bar, where dozens of leather canteens waited to be refilled; dropped Elanis's bag onto Nelis's usual stool; and hopped onto his.

The tavern fell silent. Shite! He'd thought Elanis was right behind him.

She stood straight-backed at the entrance. "Ladies and gentlemen of Teallaigh Te, I am Elanis Kimball, a mage from the Tower of Trône d'Argent." Grumbling began to drown her out. A few chairs scooted back. Veen shot to his feet, but his hand on the concealed Heart held him in place. His other hand habitually found his dagger.

"While I am Racinian," Elanis continued, "I salute the lowlanders' pride, independence, and your beautiful nation of Lekelith. May Rethfor ever guard your prosperity and keep your nation strong and your representation even stronger!"

The faces around the room were decidedly undecided. Veen knew he was as red as a rowan berry. His mouth soured.

Elanis addressed old Master van Echt behind the bar. "A drink! Whiskey all around, please!" All eyes turned to the village elder.

"Please!" Veen whispered at Master van Echt. Surprised to see Veen, the man's thoughts were plain on his face. When had he arrived? Where was Nelis? How did he know this woman? Finally, he surrendered a nod.

After the owner raised his thumb in the air, a few cheered. Elanis quickly added, "On my bill, of course." The cheers drowned out Veen's thumping heart.

Master Mann, one of the oldest piks in the village, got up from his table by the door and took Elanis's hand. His white hair swept past the tabletops as he guided her over to the counter where Veen sat. All the while, Mrs. Mann stood on her chair to scowl at her husband for taking the opportunity to drink beyond the limit she'd set for him years ago.

Above Mrs. Mann's hooked nose, her pale skin wrinkled into a smile when she spotted Veen. Veen shifted his weight and returned a quick wave before the woman came to see if Elanis had made an honest man out of him. A fairy trick that'd be! The gods would return long before, for both of their sakes!

Tightening his grip on his bag, Veen sidled out of Master Mann's way as the pik climbed onto his stool. Over the din of the other patrons shuffling to the pouring gold, Veen said, "Careful buying drinks in Lekelith, El. Lowlanders can bleed a king dry in hours."

Master Mann cackled proudly while he waved both hands to get Master van Echt's attention. Veen braced the stool with his foot to keep the pik from toppling over.

Coming out of the kitchen, Bernie Blake wore a puzzled expression for the commotion. The funny thing about the Blakes was that they all came in one size, but only Bernie had made that hefty build and strong jaw appealing. The woman was as much a miracle as a blessing. Relatively free of scandal, Bernie alone upheld the reputation of their family name, now that all three of her brothers had been sent to the Five Snakes prison. Her hair, an unruly mess of auburn curls, had half-unraveled from the bun at the back of her head.

Placing an empty pitcher under the keg behind Master van Echt, she caught sight of Veen. Her smile was slow and genuine. "Brighter day," she shouted. "Always is when the van Veen boys come home."

The van Veen boys. He liked the sound of that. "Grand to hear the months have left our reputation intact," Veen yelled back. "Nice to see you, Bernie."

She left the rush to Master van Echt and swiped one of the small glasses from a stack. After receiving a begrudging nod from Mrs. Mann, Bernie answered Master Mann's pleas with a quick pour of the good stuff.

"Bernie," Veen said, leaning over the bar as Elanis delivered her toast to Lekelith. "Can you see my friend settled? I'm dragging on my knees." The demand for a proper chat began forming behind her eyes. He put in, "And I need to see to my folks." Orphan to orphan, accepted and understood. Bernie tipped her glass to his and drank. "Thanks very much, thanks."

Removing Elanis's hand from Master Mann's, he placed it on her bag and said into her ear, "I'll be back late afternoon. Gods, please don't get yourself into trouble." Bernie had rounded the bar and hefted two of Elanis's bags before he finished speaking. With Elanis seen to, he helped Master Mann down and used the pik as a shield to distract his wife.

Outside, the air wet his face with a dozen kisses. It was time to go home. Veen took the bricked Temple Street to where it met the packed dirt of Cutter Road.

Before he turned uphill toward Mount Noafa, something purple down in the valley caught his eye. Out on one of the dry-stone walls shrouded in gorse bushes and their yellow flowers, a dark-skinned woman sat cross-legged, without a care for her silks blowing about in the damp like tethered birds. A ruthless wind spun the windmill sails before her but never dissuaded her admiring gaze for the construct, or perhaps the bog beyond it. The red, purple, pink, and orange bands in the tulip fields behind her were far more fetching.

The woman must have been mad. Even with the Heart of Rethfor warming his back, Veen couldn't wait to get out of this spit. At the edge of town, Master Malley's daffodils had spread to the side of the road. Veen dug around in his pocket and separated two copper feathers from the Frysta Avfall coins. He left them on the wall by the Malleys' gate and picked the renegades.

Cutting through the fields, he soon put his boots on Digger Road. The sight of his home caused him to stumble in surprise. River reed had replaced the old barley thatch. Their whitewashed stone hut had been scrubbed free of its moldering rime and freshly painted. So this was what Nelis had done. His surprise? Shutters? And glass in the windows? His brother hadn't spared any expense, which was wholly unlike Nelis. He hadn't even restacked the rocks over the door when he'd left.

Veen considered the strange lived-in and cared-for quality his home had developed as he approached the graves near the sheep meadow bending up the base of Mount Noafa.

Two memory wheels, circles of limestone inscribed by their loved ones, marked the resting place of their parents, two of the first victims in the revolution against Racine. Martyrs twelve years gone. He really should show Elanis the statues; they were a source of pride to his people and to him.

The war had left Nelis as the guardian of his seven-year-old brother, whom he'd never stopped calling Runt without their ma there to defend him. "Arsehole," Veen muttered. He clamped his fingers over his lips. "Sorry, Ma." Dividing the brilliant yellow flowers between the wheels, Veen sang a prayer on his knees. When he finished, he kissed the worn grave markers.

Then he gazed up Mount Noafa to the temple that had housed the Heart for centuries, wondering how it had been taken without stirring a fuss. He should've heard mention of it three steps off the boat. Missing lowlanders, yes. Missing relic, no. He'd ask the Wives of Rethfor himself. Later, when his muscles quit their whinging.

"I'll keep this safe," he said, patting his bag. "Please watch over Nelis." Then he stumbled closer to their home. His long skeleton key fit into the lock of the newly green door. With a jostle and a jerk, the latch sprang.

His boot thudded against the floor—proper floorboards. The once cramped main room had received as much attention as the outside, from the new cauldron in the fireplace to the bed that had replaced their bunks on the opposite wall. Veen ran a hand over the finely smoothed table near the fireplace. A true cupboard with dishes and cutlery stood where the shelves Nelis had nailed together from scraps had been.

Not everything was new, thankfully. Under half of the table, the oak bench their grandfather had given his ma after Nelis's birth had been recently polished. Carved vines wound around the back and down the rails to the hard seat. And he could still smell his home under the scent of freshly cut wood.

The rain fell heavily behind him, lulling his body to sleep where he stood. Closing the door, he wondered if the sudden downpour had dislodged the woman and her silks from her perch in the valley.

Veen wandered into the only other room in the house, his parents' room. The brown-and-white blanket his ma had quilted for Nelis had been draped over the sides of the new four-poster bed. A black recurve bow, a gift to Nelis from Teague, hung on the wall next to his ma's yew kast. So Nelis had taken the bedroom? Arsehole. Though, he supposed it was Nelis's birthright.

The tall kast squeaked when Veen opened its doors. His eyes refused to open after a long blink. He gave them a reprieve and felt around for his quilt. After his parents had died, he had taken the white-and-green treasure from their bed and had refused to part with it until his mercenary path threatened more danger than leaving it behind. It wasn't there.

Veen unbound his bag and gently wedged the Heart into the kast between two rough woolen blankets. If anywhere felt safe enough for the Heart, it was there. He closed the kast and gave it an affectionate pat.

Then he snickered at Teague's gift. Despite the hefty price Teague had paid the enchanter, the magus had been a mere novice, and his enchantment chose when to protect the bow's wielder at random. Oren and Veen had tested it once. Seven out of ten apples hit Nelis. However, ten out of ten smacks had landed on Veen's bum.

Moving back to the family room, Veen struck a fire, wishing aloud several times that Nelis was there with his fecking flaming sword. He stripped down and threw back the blankets, uncovering his parent's quilt. Forgiving Nelis a little for taking their room, he slipped inside and rubbed his legs together for warmth. With the orange light of the fire flickering through his eyelids, he pulled his parents' quilt up and let the rain lull him away.

Chapter 5: The Monk and the Midwife

Chattering woke Veen, still in a daze. Muddled, he threw his quilt back and searched the room. Reason came back to him as the dream lost its hold on his mind. A magpie tapped on the window. Shooing the bird away, he peered through the glass. Midafternoon light colored the verdant hills around the valley. The rain had vanished but would return before long.

His stomach rumbled. A meal wouldn't go amiss before seeking out the Wives at the temple. He tugged on his trousers and his rumpled green tunic. After stepping outside, Veen locked the door behind himself and pondered Nelis's motives for renovating their childhood home. He was a grown man now. Should he start searching for a place of his own?

From the newly thatched roof, the lone magpie spied. Above it, Veen studied Rethfor's Temple while ambling backward down the road. He turned away only when he heard voices, not wanting to look a fool.

Once inside The Wayward Tulip, Veen assumed his throne, enjoying the odor of baking baps.

Bernie filled canteens behind the bar. Grinning fit to burst, she released a hearty laugh for what someone seated on the far side of the room had said. The bun she had worn earlier had exploded into an unruly length of auburn curls. Through the locks, silver shone. A broad metal oval had been affixed over her shoulder by a fine leather strap. She glanced to where he stared. The sparkle left her eyes.

Pouring a steaming cup of tea, she said, "Your woman's not come down from her room yet."

"I'd wager dark will arrive before Elanis," Veen said, receiving the tea. He snatched his fingers away from the heat. "How've you been, Bernie?"

Her head hung as she leaned forward on her elbows. "I don't worry about you anymore. I'll say that."

"Things haven't improved in Teallaigh Te, eh?"

"The inn's full now. Don't know how 'twill fare for himself when they open the new temple in Aontus."

"You're worried for Master van Echt?" Veen asked. "That grump could survive in Frysta Avfall, trust me on that now."

"No," she answered. "I probably should do, so I should." She brushed her hair back to display the silver buckle. "You see this? Dundy sent it to me."

"Dundy?" He remembered Bernie's middle brother quite fondly, having learned to read at his side. Dundy had been the only one of Nelis's friends who'd treated him like a friend, too. But the last he'd heard, all three of the Blake brothers were in the Five Snakes. Veen bolted upright. "Bernie, did he—"

"Whisht!" she said with a quick look around. "Aye, he's escaped. Told me so in a letter that came with this." Her face drooped. "Thing is . . . you know, Dundy and Nelis's friend, Tabbira?"

He remembered Tabbi Clotts. "Raven hair. Gray eyes. Would burst into flame if the truth touched her lips."

Taking a deep inhale, Bernie agreed. "That's just the thing. She told me this morning that she met with Dundy last night, that my brother was here in Teallaigh Te, that he'd come to see me." Her nerves made her put her hands on her hips as she looked about the tavern.

"I'm not following ya. Did you not want to see him?"

"You know I do, Little Stille," she said, "so hush and listen. Tabbi said that when she was heading back to the temple she saw him get taken, just like the other lowlanders that've gone missing. You've heard about that?"

Squinting, Veen said, "Bernie, you know yourself, if bullshite were music, Tabbi'd be a grand band. A right Aunt Sheryl, she is."

"That is my concern, so. Says I to her, 'I can't tell what you're on about, Tabbi.' And she says Rethfor knows the truth and that's what matters. For all I know, the whole thing's a ruse. Yet the letter appeared to be from Dundy's hand."

Bright sunlight interrupted the gossiping whispers of the Tulip's patrons. The stranger he'd seen at the windmill stood in the entry, her skin as rich brown as rosewood. Lilac silks fluttered in the slightest breeze where not weighed down by her pink, purple, and coral bead necklaces. Her presence was pure panacea. "Who is that?" Veen asked.

"New guest, three days on. Gbad'Wu. Sweet as fresh honey, that one. Said she'd help find the truth around Dundy."

"You told her? A stranger?"

"Aye," Bernie answered, waving for the woman to join them. "Not many I'd trust with all of that. Get to know her." She ended her explanation as the stranger drew near.

Gbad'Wu tucked a spiral of her chin-length black tresses behind her ear and smirked at him without parting her full lips. She seemed to have found an answer to a riddle.

"This one is a mercenary with the Hook guild," Bernie said. "He'll give ya more interesting stories than the rest of this lot."

"Ach, I'm not that interesting," Veen deflected.

The woman perched on the stool next to him, bringing a pleasing aura of hyacinth. "The Hook has their intrigues; I am certain." Her accent was more Daijon than anything he could identify. He'd not heard an accent from the desert regions on a woman's voice before. "But I suspect you are more than a mercenary, as I am more than a midwife."

"I'll get you some tea while youse get acquainted," Bernie said. For Veen, she added, "Don't tell all your new tales, you. I want to hear them myself."

"Merci, Hibernia," the midwife said.

Bernie jerked back around. "Who told you to call me that?"

"I am sorry?"

"In all of my memories, 'twas only my gran who called me Hibernia."

"Oh, excusez-moi. What would you prefer?"

Veen was about to answer when Bernie said, "No. 'Tis good to hear it again." Wistfully, she rubbed the buckle on her shoulder. "And from your tongue it sounds pretty."

As Bernie entered the Tulip's kitchen, an apology lingered on Gbad'Wu's expression. She unwound the silken scarf from her shoulders with hands that owned more scars than Veen would expect from a woman in silks.

"Your people are very polite," she said. "I offend them and they act as though they are to blame."

Blowing air through his nostrils, he nodded. "If she brings back honey with the tea, you've done no harm."

The midwife smiled sadly. "It makes my visit difficult. I had hoped to learn more about your culture while in Lekelith. Yet every lowlander I meet is more interested in accommodating me and apologizing. Will you do me the honor of forthright conversation?"

"I've managed some horrid true honesty in my day," Veen teased. "Though, it sounds like you've already learned our culture, yeah?" He gave her skepticism a toothy grin and rapped his knuckles on the bar. "If you really want to learn our ways, you'll need to start with the nectar of our god, whiskey. They say when it goes in, the truth comes out."

Her eyes brightened. "Mais oui! I have heard the best spirits in Lekelith are in the countryside. Brewed by magpie fairies for the covens in the bogs."

The owner of The Wayward Tulip, ol' Hemshire van Echt, a far cry from a magpie fairy, tapped the dottle out of his pipe and pocketed it before waddling near. "Back already, miss? What can I get you? Better company?" He winked at Veen.

"Two drams," Veen said. "Peat-burners."

"Peat-burners?" The innkeeper tutted. "That won't do, boy, not for this breath of fresh air." He disappeared beneath the bar, then stood with a small cask in his plump hands. He patted the cask. "Now this, this is special. Triple distilled. Fifty years old, my good woman." He fiddled with the spigot and generously filled three toty wooden cups to the brim.

Master van Echt set two cups before them. "You keep this quiet, Little Stille." He tapped his cup to Veen's. "For your folks. Go on, now. The gods have had their share of this gold. Time we took ours."

Veen tapped his cup to the midwife's. Then he tossed it back quickly, anxious to witness her reaction. The strong odor had put up unnecessary defenses. Without burning, the smooth gold washed the flavors of toasted wood and smoky peat through his mouth before coating his throat.

Master van Echt wore a satisfied smile for his cup. "Worth the wait."

A gentle moan escaped Gbad'Wu, who held her chin up and her eyes closed. When they opened, adoration for Master van Echt filled them. "You have spoiled me, Master van Echt. I will never be able to taste another whiskey without disappointment." Her hand lit on Veen's forearm. "An excellent recommendation from you both. Now, what should we have for a meal? A local favorite, please."

"Tripe and drisheen!" Master van Echt proclaimed.

Veen sneered. "Ach, no, Master van Echt. You can't serve her that."

"You do not care for it?" Gbad'Wu asked.

"Never had it. But 'tis made of—"

"Do not tell me!" she said. "We will take two. Little Stille will have to be braver than I since he already knows the secret ingredients."

Veen searched for a polite decline, but Master van Echt promised, "'Twon't be long. I started a batch this morning."

The midwife laughed at Veen when he slumped forward. "'Be bold in your tenets, and the world rests in safe hands,'" she said. The highest of Rethfor's commands dripped sweetly from her lips. How lucky a babe must be to see those brown eyes upon entering this cold world.

"Gbad'Wu," she said, placing her hand on the beads over her chest. "Enchanté, Little Stille."

"Veen, please." He narrowed one eye at her. "So let me guess. In Daijon, the Hook's known as a guild of backstabbers and thieves?"

She tilted her head from side to side and admitted, "Often. Yet I am willing to give you the opportunity to prove yourself. Is it true you receive magical weapons upon completion of your guild's initiation?"

"Aye, some. The winnings are low magic, common trinkets and the like. As you travel, you find replacements fiercer than our rewards from completing the trials, or so they say."

"Your travels must differ greatly from mine," she replied. "I have only found a deficit—is that the word? A loss of magic."

"Not sure about that." Elanis might know what she meant. Eager to keep the conversation going, he said, "I met a Daijon once. A right prick, really."

If she took offense, she didn't show it, merely tucked her hair behind her ear again. "Far be it for me to tell a lowlander how stolen lands can taint your opinion of others. The history of both of my parents' people. My father was Daijon. My mother was Creb. Is it no wonder I wander?"

Creb? She should have as much trust of Racine as the lowlanders do. Driven off the lands now in south Racine, the Crebs had actually given the Lekelithians the notion to fight back, even though they had failed. Her mother must have given Gbad'Wu the bump that interrupted the smooth descent of her nose.

"One element of your guild evades a satisfactory answer," she said. "Is death a tool you frequently wield?"

He stuck his finger in his cup and spun it around on the counter. "Not often."

"May I ask how many lives you have taken?"

"A handful." He felt her waiting for more. Happy to leave it at that, he said, "Bernie tells me you're helping to find her brother."

"I will do what I can. Rumors are little to act on. Details scarcer still. All of the victims were orphans of the war. All taken from villages near Aontus in the middle of the night." She shrugged. Then a thought turned her to him. "You are a mercenary, a soldier of sorts? And you are a lowlander. Join me to question the Wives at the Temple."

Tempted to address the "of sorts," he instead asked, "Going to have a chat with Tabbi?"

"Oui. Between the two of us," she swayed near him, "we may not intimidate her."

Veen sat up. "Are you calling me short?" Gbad'Wu's laugh warmed him only slightly less than the whiskey. "Aye, I was heading there myself." He quit playing with his cup, afraid of what the Wives would admit regarding the misplaced Heart. "'Tis a day full of serious bad omens, yeah? I pray drisheen is what they're warning me of."

"Bad omens?"

"Everywhere I go, there's a magpie staring at me. Always the one." He explained, "One for sorrow."

She splayed her hands. "Another delightful find in this country. The people believe in omens."

"You ask me for help and then laugh at me."

"Not at all. Omens guide souls who are open to direction. Remember what I said about tenets—what your god said about tenets. If only in your honorable convictions do you find yourself, you still thrive." She joined her hands on the counter. "Food and travel fill in the rest quite well."

Veen chuckled and said, "Never heard of a traveling midwife before. Gladdy Mann may take offense at your arrival. I have to admit I'd like to see that."

"True midwifery," she muttered, "is best left to those more experienced." Her mouth pursed in anticipation of his question, then waited with a mirthful grin.

"If," Veen started slowly, dragging out her grin, "that is true, what job brings you here, Gbad'Wu?"

"An excellent, if difficult, question." She eyed him. "I am a midwife for the Ukresti of the Mount. Have you heard of Ukrestian monks?"

He waited for her jester's mask to crack.

Instead, her eyes wandered over the other patrons. "Then I will spare you the details. In short, I find broken souls and bring them to the Mount to be forged anew."

"You're a soul forger?" he asked. "I can see why you'd say 'midwife.'"

"No, Veen. I am a midwife. The wounded must mend themselves. I deliver them to a shelter, where their healing is guided." She lowered her chin without looking his way. "I acknowledge your disbelief."

"No disrespect meant. Honest. But you're a monk seeking recruits, yeah? In Teallaigh Te?"

Her face directed his attention to Master van Echt and welcomed the innkeeper's offering with an easy smile. Tin plates settled before them. Veen frowned at his. A white slab of stomach and a few thick, dark links. The man had been generous again.

When Master van Echt had waddled out of earshot, Gbad'Wu asked,

"Sausages? This is what you have been fearing?"

"Nelis hates it," Veen answered. "My brother, Nelis."

She cut a hearty sample from the link and put it in her mouth without hesitation. Chewing, the monk bowed her head to Master van Echt's watchful eye across the room.

The gruffest man in Lekelith practically beamed. "I say the secret's the tansy!" he shouted.

Gbad'Wu pointed her knife at Veen's plate. "Go on."

With an unsteady hand, Veen lifted a portion of the dark red blood meat. A small piece invaded his sneer. Not thinking about it being cow's blood and pig's blood and oatmeal, he chewed. Not thinking it. On the whole, it wasn't too bad, probably saved by being crisply burned, certainly saved by the saltiness.

"They salt the blood to keep it liquid," Gbad'Wu said just before he swallowed, which made it next to impossible. "Blood sausages are not my favorite, but nothing to dread. I ate pig's trotters last night."

"Crubeens," Veen said. "Those I don't mind."

Her eyebrows rose. "There is hope for you. And Nelis? Your brother."

"Heh, no. He's an oysters-and-ale man."

"Ah," she said. "Returning to what we spoke of earlier, I try to assist any community when I might deprive them of one of their own. There is a balance to it.

"While I do not worship Rethfor, I feel an affinity for his followers. If I can assist the lowlanders, I will."

More interested in solving his own mysteries around the Heart than the tripe Gbad'Wu was certain to force on him, Veen pushed his plate away and stood. "Then let's go to the temple now. I want to hear what Tabbi witnessed while 'tis fresh on her mind, yeah?"

Gbad'Wu swallowed. "Be that as it may, you've not finished your meal."

He winced apologetically.

"Very well. Give me one moment to work on mine. I've no intention of offending Master van Echt." Her heel kicked his stool. "Please sit. Tell me of your village while you wait."

Slumping over the bar, he took up his tea, which had cooled. "Teallaigh Te is beautiful. But these days, it makes me feel small."

Bernie returned in time to hear him. She set a teacup in front of Gbad'Wu and gave Veen a worried look as she presented the honeypot.

He released a small laugh. "Suppose I am at that."

Placing her knife on her plate, the monk adopted a serious expression. "Your size reflects nothing and gives no measurement to your impact on the world around you. Impact, like the bravery it requires, is wholly within your control." She resumed eating before playfully adding, "Also, you should be warned, you are my size."

The door slammed open, saving Veen from taking a bite. Grinning like a child at the Winter Peak fete, Master Mann ran to the bar and stood on the footrest to peer over. The pik's wily white eyebrows arched at Bernie from the other side of the counter.

"And where's the missus?" Bernie asked him. "You've another hour of cutting before you're to come here, Willem."

Hemming and hawing, Master Mann whined as he pulled his chest over the bar. His fingers inched their way toward a glass.

Master van Echt came to Bernie's defense. "Now, Willem, you know yourself we'd all incur Gladdy's wrath just for letting you in here at this time of day."

Amid the distraction, Gbad'Wu stabbed the sausage Veen had already cut and plopped it onto her plate. She winked at him. "You tried it. That is all I would ask."

Feeling wasteful, Veen pulled his plate to him and cut a small piece of the tripe. Gbad'Wu's covert smirk rewarded his chewing. He kept the stomach off his tongue until he felt brave enough to swallow.

Her nose wrinkled when she sampled the white organ. Veen silently thanked the gods.

Master Mann flounced onto a barstool, pleading for just a wee dram. When Bernie rounded the bar to escort the man out herself, the pik held the stool firmly to his bum.

Veen repaid Gbad'Wu's kindness and split her tripe. He tucked the larger portion into his pocket, and promised himself a thorough laundering later.

Easier to tolerate with each chewy mouthful, the tripe had nearly vanished from his plate when he looked away from Bernie's successful, if surprisingly gentle, ejection.

"Back to the bog with you!" Bernie yelled. She shared a chortle with Master van Echt when she came back around the bar. "Bless him."

Gbad'Wu moaned in defeat, gaining Master van Echt's attention. "I do not believe we are large enough to finish such wonderful generosity. Veen, perhaps you would accompany me for a walk to the temple?"

Rising too fast, Veen knocked over his stool. With all the decorum he could muster with a bulging pocket of tripe, he escorted Gbad'Wu out to the road and into the country scent of burning peat.

After he tossed the tripe to the Tulip's sunbathing cats, Gbad'Wu set their path for the village square. "Perhaps the disappearance is related to those who enjoy tripe? If so, do not worry. I will protect you."

Veen snorted. "I'm sure you've seen some things in your travels, Gbad'Wu. But this boggytrotter enjoying tripe is not one of them."

As she laughed, his vision caught on the pale beads interwoven into a larger necklace on her chest. "Did the Daijon you met explain their meaning?" she asked.

His cheeks warmed. He averted his gaze. "That arsehole was too busy leaving me for dead to discuss his trinkets."

She shook her head slightly, seeking an explanation.

"Ach, the trials were a long time ago now. I know the colors speak a language."

"You mean their order and the way they lie. I have three with the same message in different colors. One for each outfit I carry."

He took a few steps before prompting her. "Go on now. What do they say?"

She replied, "Their words are not mine to share."

His mind turned to another matter when they rounded the corner to the square where his parents' statues occupied the highest pedestal in Teallaigh Te. With the luck the magpie had been telling him of, he surrendered to Gbad'Wu's intrigue and strolled after her to his ma and da.

Bronze safeguarded their faces for his memories. They said time would take their smiles with his pain, and that's the way it was meant to be. Never. He repeated what slivers he could recall every day. Their voices. Their scents. Peat and pipe. Plump bread pulled from the heat amid a soft, lilting tune.

Gbad'Wu read the plaque aloud. "'The martyrs of Teallaigh Te and saviors of the Heart of Rethfor. May he always save room at his hearth for the first to fall, Stille and Iona van Veen.'" Her brown eyes swept over to him. "Veen? 'Little Stille'?"

With a simple, "Aye," he carried on. He felt her eyes on him until she walked by his side.

As they ascended Mount Noafa, where the overused bricks had broken away, leaving mud puddles, Gbad'Wu said, "They are a love poem." Her fingers brushed the beaded necklaces. "My father gave this to my mother the day I was born."

Midway to the wounded temple, Gbad'Wu paused to view Teallaigh Te. More clouds had rolled in to wet the air and dim the valley. "We are more kindred than appearances allow, if you can believe that. This place—so many orphans . . . I should have known why I felt at home in a country with no dunes or plains."

She gestured toward Rethfor's home. The seven braziers that had survived the Racinian assault provided a ring of warmth for the entry. "Shall we see who is preying on those who share our story?"

Chapter 6: Lies and Other Adornments

The inside of the temple pained Veen. He'd imagined the scene of his parents' demise everywhere from the catacombs to the raised hearth in the center of the sanctuary he and Gbad'Wu now stood in.

On the hearth, visible heat rose from the giant brazier. Only it had been restored after the war. Teallaigh Te had scraped together the means to erect a series of canvas tarpaulins stretching between the broken buttresses to shield the flames from the seasonal spits.

Standing on the top level of the hearth in their red robes, nine Wives of Rethfor, eyes closed and heads bowed in prayer, held hands in a circle around the brazier. Veen couldn't understand why; the Heart had vacated its fiery nest.

From an alcove leading to one of the many prayer rooms on their right, an older Wife emerged. Wife Julienne squeezed a small gold pendant on her necklace between her lips, as she did when she was troubled. Upon recognizing Veen, she released her necklace and smiled warmly. "May I help ye, children?"

Gbad'Wu answered, "Yes, sister—"

"Wife," Veen corrected. "Rethfor has Wives."

"Ah, oui," the midwife uttered. She dipped her head in thanks. "Wife? We are seeking one of your cloth. Tabbira?"

Assuming a reprimanding stance he'd seen far too often, Wife Julienne glared at nothing. "Ye'll find her in the catacombs." Her open hand gestured to the stairs past the hearth at the end of the sanctuary.

Veen had taken five steps before he realized Gbad'Wu didn't follow. She said to Wife Julienne, "You do not seem pleased we have asked for her audience."

Keeping an eye on the other Wives, Wife Julienne quietly replied, "Tabbira has always been a fanciful creature. If this tale of witnessing an abduction—two abductions now—does not endear her to Rethfor, as I must assume she hopes it does, at least she'll receive plenty of attention while her next tale forms."

"Two abductions?" Veen asked. "Did she see who took them?"

With a deep sigh, Wife Julienne kindly directed them to the catacombs again. "You had better ask her, Little Stille. I'd prefer not to mislead you by misspeaking or spreading falsehoods."

Rainwater evaded the tarpaulins to dampen the stone steps, puddled in divots, and trickled down to the musty, earthy catacombs. Oil lamps lit five passages branching away to twist out of sight in the distance. Gbad'Wu skewed her lips and studied their options.

"Not exactly a cave, no?" Veen asked.

"No. I should say not. Where do we begin our search?"

Veen thought for a moment. "I think I know. C'mon."

Taking the first tunnel on their right, they ventured deeper through the full dark and interrupting dim light of the sparse oil lamps. Several minutes passed before they reached a two-story room. Stacked openings had long ago been stuffed full of neatly arranged bones.

He hated this place. Always had. Nelis and his friends had come here sometimes when grooming their mischief. Fresh from his memory, Tabbira puffed on her pipe while seated on a casket in the corner. Its odor wasn't one shared by any pipe in The Wayward Tulip or the Mercantile Guild hall.

Unable to resist, Veen yelled, "Tabbi-Tabbi-Tall-Tales!"

Lekelithian temper colored her face as she leaped to her feet. It didn't cool when she recognized him. She had enjoyed Nelis's company but had only tolerated his. "You will remember your surroundings, boyo," she shouted back and brushed her black hair over her shoulder. Then, catching herself, she softened her voice, "This is a place of rest, child."

Gbad'Wu looked askance at him. "Please accept our apologies for intruding, Wife of Rethfor. We have sought you out to ask for your assistance."

Donning the air of a Wife rather than a holy terror, Tabbi tapped out her pipe and hid it away in her robes before steepling her hands under her chest. "How might I help youse, children?"

"Stop calling us 'children' for one," Veen grumbled.

She pointedly ignored him.

"We heard you have witnessed the abduction of Dundy Blake," Gbad'Wu said.

"A tragedy," Tabbi replied.

Inclining her head for more, Gbad'Wu finally said, "Yes. Well, we were hoping you could relay your tale for us."

Laying her hand over her heart, Tabbi dipped into a small curtsy. "I saw it. But I'm sorry to say youse will not find him. The very power of the gods, of my husband, has taken him to the Glades."

Gbad'Wu raised an eyebrow. "Please, explain."

Tabbi presented some folded parchment from her robes and passed it to Gbad'Wu. "Last night, Dundy sent me a message. He asked me to meet with him in the valley near the mill. He was conflicted over the way he had gained his freedom and needed some wisdom, the perspective of Rethfor's Wives."

Veen rolled his eyes.

"As I left him, he thanked me and said he'd decided to do what's right. But not before he saw his little sister again. I was so very proud of him."

Sinking back down to the casket, Tabbi spoke to her hands. "At the top of Mount Noafa, something told me to go to the edge. In the valley, the light, green like the Glades themselves, swallowed him. He vanished. You see, Dundy sits at Rethfor's side now."

Veen shifted his weight. "And the other one? Wife Julienne said you witnessed two abductions."

"My cousin in Piddlebo," she said sadly. "The same."

Gbad'Wu scoffed, returning some of the red to Tabbi's face. "A green light? That is what you saw? Nothing else? No sounds? No smells?"

"I can't smell the valley from up here, can I?" Tabbi said before remembering to add a patronizing, "Child."

The monk turned to go.

"Oh, but . . ." Tabbi waited for Gbad'Wu's full attention. "Now that you mention it, there was a crackle. Louder than a fire, but similar."

"Merci. Au revoir," Gbad'Wu said and gave Veen's sleeve a tug.

"Yes," Tabbi said. "I must return to my prayers."

Aggravatingly, Wife Julienne wasn't around to answer Veen's questions about the Heart when they returned to the sanctuary. Gbad'Wu didn't slow regardless. He'd have to come back after their evening prayers.

Outside, it had become a grand soft day with a misting rain. Gbad'Wu went to the edge of Mount Noafa. "From here, can you see a man in the valley?"

Veen considered it.

"At night?"

Thinking as he spoke, Veen answered, "If the green light was bright enough, perhaps."

The monk made a face at him. "You believe her?"

He shrugged. "My band doesn't keep me around to do the thinking."

Gbad'Wu placed a hand on her hip. "Fools are not rumored to be counted in the Hook's numbers."

"You'd be surprised."

Her dark eyes doubted him or said she'd found the fool herself. Either way, she wandered on.

"I don't believe her full story. But something about it rings true, Gbad'Wu. And we don't have any proof she's lying, either."

"No," the monk admitted. "But you'll find perception creates more truths than facts. And for her, my perception says the first Wife we met held more accuracy in her words."

Veen thought while they descended Mount Noafa. "This strange light and crackle have to be magic, yeah?"

She nodded slightly.

"My friend, Elanis, she could sense it."

"Even if the abduction was hours ago?" Gbad'Wu asked.

Raising a shoulder, he put his hands out. "Let's find out. Tabbi may not be the end of our trail to Dundy."

At the inn, Elanis answered her door fully dressed. "I was just about to eat. Are you hungry?" The mage regained her proper posture for the stranger standing with Veen.

"El." Veen turned to Gbad'Wu. "I'm not sure where to begin."

"Perhaps with an introduction. Gbad'Wu." The monk dipped into a curtsy.

After Elanis mirrored the pleasantry, she let them enter. Lavender and cinnamon scented the air in the small inn room. On the writing table, four pouches huddled around a mortar and pestle like hungry baby birds. Gbad'Wu explained Tabbi's tale before the three of them set off for the valley near the mill.

Taking in the vibrant bands of tulips, Elanis said, "Beautiful, just beautiful." Closer to the windmill, she paced near the yellow coconut-scented flowers of the gorse bushes and pursed her lips. "If something like that had happened, I do believe I'd still sense it. The spell does sound quite powerful."

Gbad'Wu shot Veen a look calling Tabbi a liar.

"Are you sure this is where he was abducted?" Elanis asked.

Veen kicked back some of the bushes, searching for signs Tabbi may have told the truth for once. "'Tis what Tabbi said. Somewhere around here, within sight of the ledge on Mount Noafa."

Elanis sidestepped to her left until she reached a dry-stone wall and searched about. "I'm sorry; I sense nothing."

Bernie bustled down the path from town toward them. "What did Tabbi say? Did you speak with her?"

Trapped between admonishment of Tabbi and defeating Bernie's hope, Gbad'Wu answered, "Let me tell you over a cup of tea."

"Oh gods, yes," Elanis moaned. "I'd eat a lamb raw if it came too close."

At The Wayward Tulip, Veen coaxed Elanis away from the others to a table in the corner. He didn't envy Gbad'Wu's position. Bernie may not have seen Dundy in years, but the man was her brother and a kind soul when sorted.

Elanis peered out the nearby window and said, "Oren has surely told Nelis and Teague by now."

Veen's gut churned. "You say such things!"

"Don't worry about your gormless brother, Veen. Teague can force reason through his thick skull." She reassured herself with a nod. "He may still tan your hide for putting yourself in that kind of danger—or for jeopardizing the plan—or for listening to me."

"Not helping, El. I know he'll understand about the Heart. He'd have done the same. 'Tis the deviation from his plan that'll have me standing for a year. And what he feels we owe Mage Curtiss worries me, so." He glanced about them to make sure no one listened. "The temple failed to protect the Heart. Who are we supposed to trust it to now? I'll die before handing it over to a Tower or the temple."

The conversation between Gbad'Wu and Bernie ended sooner than Veen expected. Less disappointed than flushed with anger, Bernie busied herself behind the bar. Now he wished he'd joined them. Gbad'Wu retreated upstairs.

"It's safe," Elanis said.

"Not safe enough."

A savory scent started Veen's mouth watering. Bernie had loaded her arms full. "There you go now. Stew and two teas."

Receiving her cup of cha and a bowl of beef stew with suet dumplings, Elanis said, "You, my lady, are a rubious goddess."

Bernie giggled. "You should teach these peat-cutters a thing or two about complimenting a lady. I wouldn't mind hearing that in a baritone now and then." She laid down a spoon for Elanis and said, "I'll see you have a glass of frost wine for that. My treat."

Warming his fingers on his cup while he ogled Elanis's stew, Veen said, "Bernie, could I—"

She held her hand up. "I was wondering if you'd admit to wasting your food earlier."

Veen cringed. "Ach. Was it obvious?"

"Mm-hmm. But don't you worry. Himself didn't notice." One deep sigh with her hands on her hips and he was off the hook. "I'll be back in a moment."

When Bernie left, Elanis said, "Tell me. Why do I suspect this particular relic means more to you than any other of Rethfor's faithful?"

His cheeks warmed. "I never—'tisn't something—Nelis thought we shouldn't tell you . . . I mean, I agreed." He took a deep breath and set his cup down. "Ach, fine. You know how the revolt started? What ignited the war?"

Elanis gave the polite Racinian response. "The lowlanders were duly tired of being taxed by the merchants and the king."

"Too true. But the spark to the blaze? What bound the people together?" He leaned back from the table and crossed his arms while Bernie delivered his meal, with an extra dumpling. Blessedly, Master Mann ran inside and straight to the bar, drawing her away again. "King Clyde's men came after the Heart."

"No!" Elanis said with whispered shock. "I've met King Clyde; he'd never do such an unscrupulous thing."

"Truer than my lineage, he did. El, my ma and da died keeping the Heart out of his hands." That cleared her expression. "A rider from Aontus warned the lowlanders that their peaceful struggle had ended. That night, soldiers stormed Teallaigh Te." He looked over to the bar. "My parents and ol' Master van Echt went to guard the Heart. But they were late. One of the merchants owned by the crown had already sent his guards to slay the Wives and steal the relic." His voice tremored. "My ma put the Heart in Master van Echt's hands and told him to run. He escaped through the catacombs while they held off Racine's soldiers. Then the magi burned the temple."

Awkwardness always accompanied that story. Before Elanis could say something silly like an apology, he spoke. "Anyroads, once the treaty was signed, Master van Echt let the Wives of Rethfor restore it to the flames in the temple." He absentmindedly emptied his bowl.

A vacancy lingered in Elanis's eyes. "That's why Nelis raised you. I didn't realize you were so young. You couldn't have been more than eight."

Seven, he thought. But he nodded, wondering if the tale had actually endeared Nelis to her.

Elanis curled her finger against her mouth as she chewed and thought. She swallowed. "I won't speak ill of my king, being Ameera's father, but the threat of losing that kind of power—"

Veen slammed his spoon down. "Won't speak ill of him? He killed my parents!" Elanis shook her head, but he knew what defense was coming. "Will you snuff out that feckin' candle already? There are more women out there than the dreaded princess. Some that'll remember you're there when they don't need you. 'Tis no wonder Nelis doesn't trust you, no?"

The hurt entered her eyes before she corrected her posture and gazed into the middle distance out the window.

He pushed himself up from the table and took a stool at the bar. "Ale, red or darker," he said to Bernie. "Please."

Darkness had overtaken the window before he felt himself calm. The patrons had left him alone for the most part, must've sensed he'd run them through for interrupting his thoughts. Elanis sat alone as well. She had finished her meal and received a second frost wine. The mage never took her eyes off the window.

With a deep inhale, Veen slipped off his stool and nearly spilled his pint on Gbad'Wu. Gods, she was quiet! "I, em, I'm sorry. I owe you, for the meal. For earlier. Bernie—"

"No, no," she said. A smile relayed the monk's approval. "I am better for having met you, Veen. Please take that as a good omen."

Veen walked tall to El's table, blaming his pint for his flushed face. "She's pretty," Elanis said. "No magic. That's a shame."

"No crown either." He winced.

Elanis gave a brief, humorless laugh.

He shrugged an apology and sat. "She's interesting. A monk. Ukresti's Mount or something."

"A monk in rural Lekelith? Why?"

"Traveler," he answered. "She's getting herself involved in the search for the missing villagers while seeking recruits. That's all I know."

Elanis lowered her wine. "Veen, what I was going to say earlier, it's so much more than loyalty to the crown." She scooted forward. "Rumors . . . In the Tower, Ameera, Jean, and I found a tome from—gods know—ages ago—easily the time of the elves. It's what started—no, forget that. My point is the tome said a relic—a true god's relic—added to any spell can create a miracle. Or a catastrophe. It posits I alone could burn Aontus to cinders in seconds." Her fingers splayed before him for emphasis.

"Shite," Veen breathed, sinking back into his chair.

"Oh, yes. Shite." She took another pull before saying, "I don't know the truth of it, of course. However, the evidence in that tome convinced the three of us. It said Merith had sought the relics out. With one spell, the relic was gone forever, and with it, their opposition. It explains how they overthrew a continent in ten years, among other things. And how the lowlanders still have their relic; Merith never conquered your people because the lowlanders kept leaving their lands to avoid them. By the time the Revolt of the Magi ended Merith, no one knew they should hide their relics.

"So, no. Under absolutely no circumstances shall we give the Heart to a Tower or to a country."

Stunned, he didn't know what to say, and Elanis stopped meeting his eyes. "There's more, El. Those men at the Boyd Estate, they were working with King Clyde."

"Why? Because they mentioned a king? Yes, I heard it. But bear in mind Merith had a king, too. I suspect that king has more hold over the Filii Cinere than mine does."

"Maybe, definitely maybe." Convinced enough to share, he said, "I overheard something else. A Racinian named Harold left for Trône d'Argent today, seeking a cache somewhere outside the city. I don't know what it means."

Elanis paled. "A Merithian cache?"

Veen shrugged.

Surprisingly, she smiled. "Not our concern. A Racinian named Harold who associates with the Boyds of Aontus and has arrived in Trône d'Argent today needs men and supplies to uncover this 'cache.' That should be plenty for Ameera to go on."

"Ameera?" Veen asked. "She'll get your message too late. What if they collar her?"

"Veen," Elanis said with a laugh, "we're magi. She'll have my message before her maidens undress her for the night, well before Harold has left the city." He didn't know what that meant, but Elanis rose with her iron goblet and without explanation or concern. "Well," she said, "it's a loathsome job, but someone must drink with the alluring woman."

He stood, wearing an apology on his face. She looked away from it. "I'll see to the stone," he said.

"Breakfast?" she asked.

"Aye. Of course." Her hand patted him twice on the back before she left him.

Dropping a few coins on the counter, he wished Bernie a good night. Then he strode on home. The half-moon bordered fluffs of broken clouds. As he repeated the journey he'd taken a thousand times, his drink stirred a song in him.

The song halted when a shadow moved across the window in his home. Drawing the black steel daggers from his belt, he crept forward to the window. Oren sat the table. "Bugger, bugger, bugger." Sucking in all the air he could muster, Veen drew himself up to face Nelis. He exhaled and charged inside.

Upon seeing him, Oren stood. No Nelis. No Teague.

"Where is El?" Oren asked.

"Where's Nelis?" Veen asked.

His answer flung the front door open behind him. Nelis grabbed Veen's tunic. Veen kicked for the floor as his brother lugged him to the wall and crushed him against it. "Youse did what?"

"We saved the Heart of Rethfor!" Veen shouted as he squirmed in vain. "From a feckin' cult!"

His feet still dangling, Veen slid down the coarse wall until his eyes stared evenly at the beast Nelis held within. "Where is it, Runt?"

"Safe," Veen said with a pained crack in his voice. Expecting the beast to roar, Veen winced. He nearly fell over when his feet hit the floor.

Nelis fixed him with a murderous snarl. "I know where it is," his brother said and, with a snap of his fingers, stormed outside.

"Elanis doesn't have it!" Veen yelled. Nelis would tear open whatever had healed of the fresh wound Veen had left in the mage. "Oren, Elanis doesn't have the Heart. Don't let him do this!" Lost in uncertainty, the Caperi didn't budge. Veen huffed.

Sprinting as fast as he could, Veen didn't make it in time to stop the thundering storm of his brother. Light fell on Nelis as he threw open the doors to the Tulip. When Veen caught up, Bernie was flummoxed and rounding the bar, watching the furious inches between Elanis and Nelis. Elanis's mantle lay crumpled at her feet. Her spectacles had come off with it. Gbad'Wu and everyone else around the crowded tavern stood and watched their posturing with concern.

"Give it back!" Nelis demanded. He redirected his anger to Veen. "You trusted it to this witch?"

Elanis's palm smacked Nelis's bald head. His hands throttled her forearms. "You know," she said coolly, "hitherto, you've been tolerable. But now, Nelis, I must admit with fervor you are a vast and mighty arsehole."

Nelis's snarling lip reached its limit.

A brown hand appeared between their red faces. Tiny Gbad'Wu forced herself between them. "You are Nelis?"

Nelis furrowed his brow at her.

"Yes. Veen can express himself in words. So, I must assume you are capable." She bent to return Elanis's belongings to her.

Hands on her hips, cheeks pink, Bernie glowered at Nelis like a bull ready to gore. Her throat cleared.

Nelis took a step back. "Sorry, Bernie. But this is important."

Flinging her arms out, Elanis said, "Your riving frenzy has piqued everyone's interest."

"Whatever your trouble," Master van Echt's voice rumbled, "youse take it outside. Now."

Before Elanis or Nelis budged, Wife Julienne brushed past Oren and Veen. "Help!" Her eyes widened when they landed on Nelis. "Nelis, please! Tabbira has gone missing." She ran to him and took his hand in hers, trying to pull him back with her. "In the catacombs, there's blood!"

Gbad'Wu caught Bernie's eye and pointed her chin to the stairs. Bernie obeyed without hesitation, bounding up to the inn rooms. "Please, Wife," the monk said, taking Nelis and Elanis by the wrists, "lead on swiftly."

Chapter 7: A Common Path Forward

Veen trailed behind them up Mount Noafa when he heard Bernie panting to catch up. A two-foot blade topped the spear she used as a walking stick. Though winded, she didn't slow at his side, merely choked out, "C'mon, Little Stille."

Gbad'Wu took the weapon from Bernie with a "Merci." She asked Wife Julienne, "You are certain she has not sought out a place for her herbal pursuits?"

"This is a ceremonial night," the Wife answered. "The fourth of many for Rethfor's betrothed. Tabbira would not miss it for all of the menji in Cyr." She halted for a deep inhale. "She would be stripped of her robes, child."

Bernie bounced on the balls of her feet as they gave the old woman a reprieve. Then she peeled the sweaty hair from her face and glared at Nelis. Obeying the heat of a Lekelithian woman's temper, Nelis put the Wife's arm around his shoulder and swept her off her feet. A surprised shout was the only protest the woman gave until they reached the summit, where she reprimanded him with that all-too-familiar Wife Julienne evil eye.

On flat ground, they breezed through the sanctuary, solely occupied by four Wives surrounding the brazier on the hearth, and down into the catacombs. Wife Julienne guided them along the route Gbad'Wu and Veen had taken earlier and marched to the corner where Tabbira had been smoking. "We searched for her here when she did not show for the feast." When she knelt, her bony hand brought their attention to a spattering of dried blood.

"Not more than a bad nosebleed," Veen commented. He'd hit enough noses to know that.

Oren tracked the drops into the dark. Elanis brought out her brass peacock. Dim blue light from the palm-sized bird lit the dark tunnel as they ventured inside.

Gbad'Wu laid her hand on Wife Julienne's shoulder. "We can find you in the sanctuary above?"

Defiance crinkled the Wife's eyes, but she let them delve deeper into the catacombs alone.

Squatting at a junction between three passages, Oren spread his arms to keep the others behind him. "Sandali lang. Disturb their trail and this will be more difficult."

"Their?" Gbad'Wu asked.

"Two," he answered. "Both walking."

Sweeping her arm to where Oren pointed, Elanis spread the blue light to each of the tunnels and repeated the task.

"Can't you make that thing brighter?" Nelis asked.

"You know I can't."

Abruptly, Oren rushed down the corridor to the left. Gbad'Wu and Veen stayed on his heels. Dirt walls and ancient pillars replaced the smooth stone. Bones arranged by type, not bodies, filled the holes in the walls. Above their crisscrossed yellow remnants, skulls gazed upon Tabbira's seekers. "Does this maze of death ever end?" Oren muttered when they took the second turn to the right.

Any child of Teallaigh Te would know where they were headed. "Almost there, Oren," Veen said. "This leads straight to the woods by the bog."

Fresh air and pattering stole Veen's hope. Wind throttled the treetops outside the exit. Raindrops pelted down hard enough to have already formed large puddles. Veen considered whether this storm, one so strong and fast, could be natural. He couldn't recall one like it coming to Teallaigh Te.

Nelis grabbed the Caperi's shoulder. "Don't give up! She's a friend, boy."

Rain dripped from Oren's slicked-down hair as he silently apologized to Nelis.

"Take us as far as you can," Gbad'Wu said.

Pointing to his heel, Oren lifted his foot to show her the indention. "We have arrived. The blood is gone by now. The soil soft. Branches break against each other in this storm."

Drawing his short sword, Nelis held it out. The blade blazed to orange, emitting less light than Elanis's peacock. He wandered forward.

"Nelis?" Veen called.

"No, Runt! She deserves everything we have to give."

Wordlessly, Gbad'Wu and Bernie joined Nelis's fanciful search through the woods. Elanis left the shelter of the cave with her hood up. Fanning out, they searched and shivered until they reached the edge of the water-soaked bog.

"They could only head north until here," Elanis said.

Still as a statue, Nelis observed the ringed ripples in the puddles on the bog until Gbad'Wu put her hand on his forearm, rose up on the balls of her feet to share his view, and said, "Let us meet at first light and continue our search."

He scanned the darkness for another minute before he agreed.

They found Wife Julienne kneeling at the hearth in the sanctuary. The sight of them, wet to the bone and forlorn, brought her to her feet. She studied their faces wordlessly.

"We must resume in the morning," Gbad'Wu said. She gestured to the puddles that had avoided the tarpaulins. "The rain has washed away the trail."

Weakly, Nelis asked, "Wife Julienne, is the Heart safe?"

Her eyes widened. "Of course, child. Why would you ask that?"

Veen caught her glance at Elanis's silver mantle.

"Rumors in Aontus," Nelis lied. "They say the Heart's been stolen."

Bernie gasped and let out a loud, "Gods!" She uttered a speedy apology to Wife Julienne.

"'Tisn't in any danger," the Wife said firmly. "I can assure ye, children."

"Can I see it?" Nelis asked.

Again, her eyes swept to Elanis, who in turn snorted a laugh. "I won't wrest it away from the lowlanders. If I were you, I'd be more concerned for whether I can tell an illusion resides in that altar of yours. There is the all-too-familiar tingle of a childish prank coming from up those steps where your Heart is meant to be."

"Enough," Wife Julienne relented lowly. She ushered them away from the other Wives and to the sanctuary's entrance. "My husband's relic has been taken to its new home in Aontus." She glanced up to the Wives ringing the brazier. "Yes, the Tower set an illusion in place to keep that secret from those who'd take advantage of its travels. But fear not, I have received confirmation it arrived safely. When the new temple is consecrated next week, everyone will know." She tugged Nelis's sleeve with her withered hand to turn him toward the exit. "So please save your concerns for Tabbira, child." Without a farewell, she left them.

Bernie nudged herself between Veen and Nelis. "Is the Heart really gone? It belongs in Teallaigh Te! They can't take it from us!"

"Easy, Bern," Nelis said. "So long as the Heart's safe." Safe and rightly warm in their ma's kast.

"She is right to be concerned," Gbad'Wu said, leaning against her spear. "The history of my people runs deeper than yours. A god's relic should not be without its guardians."

"You heard Wife Julienne," Nelis said. "Focus your concern on Tabbi."

With that, they left the temple and planned to meet at The Wayward Tulip at first light. "I'll have warm coddle ready for youse before the sun is," Bernie promised when she and Gbad'Wu separated from the Hook at Digger Road.

Elanis protested at being dragged by Oren toward the van Veen household, "We have a handful of hours to sleep. Can't this wait?"

Oren defeated her with a rare glare. His forefinger delivered an unspoken threat and defeated Nelis, too, before it pointed them onward. "Or should I summon Teague?"

The van Veen cottage didn't need a roaring fire to stave off the frigid late evening with Elanis and Nelis squared off at their corners of the table. Veen agreed with Oren; they needed to mend this rift. But Oren lacked Teague's finesse in bringing about a resolution.

After a moment of silence, Oren finally said, "We should have asked Clarkson for permission to search for the lowlanders ourselves."

"He'd want to know who was going to pay for it," Elanis replied.

Nelis sniffed. "Not the lowlanders. Runt and I are considered wealthy compared to our kin. Even those who joined the temple to survive aren't safe."

"That is my point," Elanis said. Yes, all of the chill was now contained within her. "The wealthy are not the targets. Due to bias and mistrust, those who cannot pay are not seeking outside assistance."

After receiving a cup of tea from Oren, she said, "I'm exhausted, so let's assuage our Caperi friend, Nelis." Belying her stony face, her voice quavered. She put her cup down without drinking. "I've tolerated your gurning and your relentless prejudice against Racine. I even understand it, much more so now."

He snorted. "You don't know what you're talking about." Veen could hear the insults forming behind his brother's brown eyes. Nelis turned his annoyance on Oren. "What's the point of this?"

"The point," Oren said, "is to admit our deeds and move onward. Teague will hear these shenanigans best without the shouting, I think. If you do not see this through, know I have secrets to use against each of you. Three on you, Bigger van Veen."

"Yes," Elanis said. "We'd hate for you to fall out of favor with Teague."

Veen suddenly felt like the tagalong again.

Red-faced, Nelis gave a slight shake of his head. "Where is the Heart?"

"The band first," Oren said, his face devoid of patience. "You nearly announced we possess the Heart to a tavern tonight. I blame your distrust."

Veen poured himself a cup. "'Tis true, Nelis," he said, receiving a flashed accusation of betrayal. "You can't even set foot in Racine proper, one of the largest nations on the continent. You make us dodge any assignments that take us within a hundred miles, yeah? 'Tis time to move past this." Veen's mouth ran on before his mind stopped it. "She's like a sister to me, Nelis. And to you too, if you had the wisdom to see it."

Oren snickered into his cup.

"Runt, you know yourself what that war cost us. Racine takes. Always from the those who've the least to give."

"What does that have to do with me?" Elanis asked. "Am I responsible for my country's political stratagems? I believe I'd recall King Clyde requesting my consult." The frost melted from her eyes. "Nelis, we were kids ourselves during that war. Yes, even you."

Nelis steepled his hands before rubbing them against his brow.

"Nelis," Elanis murmured. "I'd never betray you. Wasn't that what the Hook's trials were truly about?"

He cleared his throat. "Fine. I'm sorry." If it were a heartfelt bonding Oren sought, he'd go disappointed, for that was it. "Now, where is the Heart? Our ma died for it. 'Tis as important as family to me and Runt."

"Da, too," Veen muttered, studying a knot in the wood. Veen felt Elanis take a deep breath next to him before she nudged his arm. "In Ma's kast."

Oren got up to retrieve it.

"You hid it?" Nelis asked, dumbfounded. He arched an eyebrow at Elanis.

Elanis asked, "Didn't think I'd deny a gambit for my power-obsessed rulers? Perhaps I'm not as Racinian as you think."

Nelis smiled slightly. "Say that to Ameera."

The mage blushed. "Bite your tongue, savage."

Laying the white stone on the table, Oren said, "Your relic, Master van Veen." His fingers streaked the Heart with pink. Except Elanis, the others played their fingers over the smooth surface. Warmed head to toe through to his bones, Veen stared into the glossy relic.

"Miracle or massacre?" Elanis asked. "Which waits to be born from you?"

"What are you on about?" Nelis asked.

Elanis hid her face in her cup. Veen took his turn to nudge her. She raised her brow innocently. Veen prodded harder. "All right, you pest," she said. "I believe what Gbad'Wu had begun to explain before you rudely interrupted her is true and pertinent." Oren paled to the pasty white of Nelis as Elanis retold the tome's accusations against Merith's rapid conquests.

Nelis snatched the Heart away from her. "No offense meant."

"None taken," she replied. "I want nothing to do with it, aside from keeping it far away from those who would conjure their own apotheosis."

"Destroy a city in seconds?" Oren asked.

Removing her mantle, Elanis rose. She draped it over a ladder-back chair and scooted it closer to the fire. "Ameera proposed that's what happened to the lost dwarven city of Quinton. From the description the tome gave, it's a sound guess. The timing fits as well, around the first time the satyrs attempted to rally Shallyghal."

"Shite," Veen breathed. Fully pink in Nelis's grasp, the Heart seemed innocent enough. "You didn't tell me that. Should we maybe take it to Clarkson?"

Elanis and Oren waited for Nelis to respond. A sensible silence passed before he said, "I'll protect it. I don't trust the Wives with it. Rethfor forgive me; I don't. I don't trust the Hook with it, either. I'll watch it while you three search for Tabbi. We can decide how we'll keep it safe tomorrow, after I've had some time to think."

"But, Nelis," Veen sputtered, "she's your friend. I can—"

"The greater good, Runt. You go." His mind made up, his protective brother wouldn't relent before the time it would take for rocks to crumble and become smooth again. Nelis stood with the Heart clutched against his chest. At the entrance to his room, he paused. "Oren, El." Her nickname sounded strange on his tongue, even if there was an uncomfortable charm in the attempt. "Elanis. Watch him."

Veen shouted after him, "I defeated the feckin' minotaur!"

Whipping her mantle off the chair, Elanis gave it a good shake and brushed back the dried black hair on her forehead. "Shall we go now?" she asked Oren. Crisp air leaked in through the doorway. Brief farewells exchanged, Veen stood in the door's shelter from the chill once more.

Nelis returned, never blinking. His reprimanding stare squashed Veen back to the bench. Veen's hands shielded either side of his bum, even after Nelis sat across from him. Nelis picked up Oren's unfinished tea and drank, still watching Veen with his dark eyes. "You told Oren. Why didn't you tell me, Runt?"

Discomfort crept through Veen's chest and made his jaw tingle. He gave a halfhearted shrug.

Crossing his arms, Nelis leaned back in his chair. "I'm your brother. You're supposed to come to me when you do something stupid. Dumb. Against orders. Putting the rest of us in danger, too. Putting our employment in danger." The growl returned to his voice. "Youse two thunderin' eejits could have gotten yourselves killed. If you think 'tis bad luck to go with less than six, why'd you go with two? Two? Tempting the fae?" Nelis delivered a shaming look better than Veen could recall his ma doing.

Veen glowered and said, "Maybe if you treated me more like a nineteen-year-old mercenary and less like . . . like I'm still some small fella tagging along with your friends."

"Aye, well," Nelis said with an unpredicted grin, "that's what brothers do, Runt." He gestured to the room around them. "You think I spent my time, our money, on repairing our home so you could get yourself killed before we can enjoy it? Be a shame to go to the Glades when we just got a proper floor." The heels of his boots tapped the floorboards.

Veen smiled, despite himself.

"What did I say when we entered the Hook's trial?"

It felt like a lifetime ago. "When you had hair on that melon?" Veen asked.

Nelis smirked.

"'Just till we get our feet under us.' But, you're not suggesting we leave? To be what? Peat-cutters in Teallaigh Te?"

The enforcer of their band spread his hands around his small cup. "Don't slight them. Those are our people."

"Our people?" Veen asked. "What of our band? They need us. We can't abandon them."

Nelis snorted. "They have new trials every year, Runt. New mercs get swapped in all the time."

"You, me, Oren, Teague, Elanis, Joseb—we're family, Nelis."

Nelis put his gaze on the fire.

"How can you turn your back on them? Family means something, doesn't it?"

Nelis slammed his palms on the table and roared, "I want you living in twenty years! This stew you've got us cooking in now—" He rolled his shoulders and sat back down. "You're in no position to argue. When I say we're done, we're done. Burn me if fate doesn't already say it with what's in Ma's kast."

Veen defied his brother's authority with an angry glower. With lingering disappointment on his face, Nelis left his ideas to soak.

Alone, Veen strummed his thoughts, constructing a tune as he undressed that'd release him from Nelis's control. He'd steal from a crimson dragon before he'd leave the Hook.

In his bed, he snuggled under his ma's quilt and took comfort from the fire dancing on the hearth. His thoughts turned to Mage Curtiss. What did the mage want with the relic? "'Miracle or massacre. Which waits to be born from you?'"

A prayer to Rethfor for protection of the god's own relic ended the mercenary's day. A mercenary for life.

Chapter 8: Tattling to Teague

Plentiful clouds and muck revealed as many clues to Tabbira's abduction as the wetlands had hours earlier. Gbad'Wu's persistence had kept Oren crouched and sharp-eyed until even her patience waned in the early afternoon.

Veen stooped next to Oren at the edge of a deep stream and plucked a stone. Simple and smooth, it sang no song for Tabbira. "Getting a lot from that mayfly, are ya?"

Oren released a long sigh and stood.

Flicking mud off her thigh from a misstep, Elanis said, "If I had a vial of her blood, I could scry her location."

"A wee bit forbidden, no?" Veen asked.

Shirking the Towers' rigors as only a member of the Hook could, or perhaps a mercenary suffering an infatuation would, Elanis muttered,

"Perhaps."

"What she left won't work?" Bernie asked.

"It's dry. The blood must drip and run."

Half to herself, Gbad'Wu said, "It was dried last night." Her face turned expectantly to Veen. "Her abduction must have occurred shortly after our visit. Did you notice anything strange?"

"Ach, I said I didn't. Aside from her words, yeah?" Veen skipped the stone across the merged puddles of the quagmire. "No great flash of light this time."

Elanis added, "And not to be dispiriting, no residual magic in the moor."

"Could someone unfamiliar with your bog navigate it easily?" Gbad'Wu asked.

"No," Bernie answered. "If they dragged her through that awful strange downpour in the dark of night, they'd both have drowned. Ask any peat-cutter; not even they'll be working today."

Veen chortled and explained, "More afraid of missing a drinking day than truly sinking below the mud."

Bernie's small smile disappeared. She heaved her bosom with a long inhale. "Poor Tabbira. She was a right you-know at times, but she didn't deserve that, so."

"Few would," Gbad'Wu said. Her thoughts remained her own as she watched Elanis brushing off more of the brown crust coating her legs. Relaxing the arm holding her spear upright, the monk sighed. "Je suis désolée; I fear defeat is ours."

Considering he'd been saying it since late morning, Oren humbly nodded and led on back toward Teallaigh Te.

Bernie gave the unhelpful bog one last glance. "Right. We'll drink to her tonight."

"We should see to Nelis," Oren said to Elanis and Veen, prompting

Bernie's suspicions again.

"Must be a crippling bout of the shites to keep himself from this," Bernie said to Veen.

"That's what I said, no?" Veen replied, forgoing the smirk to Elanis for believability's sake.

"A shame that. Those two were a menace together for years. Always thought she'd marry your brother, not Rethfor."

"Wise choice," Oren said, surprising Veen. He'd never turned a whisker of mean in Nelis's direction before. Elanis giggled to herself, until a swarm of midges caused her to spit. "Given the options," he added, "a god would be hard for any man to rival."

"Never a truer word said," Bernie agreed. "I've some black tea and sugar for himself. Come to the Tulip. Youse could all do with a warm meal and a pint."

Gbad'Wu separated from them to inform Wife Julienne of their failure.

The Tulip bustled with laughing peat-cutters and wives who had decided to neglect their duties to give the men counsel and company. Everyone fell quiet when Bernie came in.

Master van Echt stopped drying a mug to hunker forward. "Well?" His head shook when hers did. "Shite. C'mon, then, Bernie. Give us a hand."

Piks and humans, men and women, focused on Bernie, waiting for more news. Assuredly, she addressed the room. "I can't say if we should raise our glasses or our prayers. Hold your guard high and hope Tabbi's just being herself again, yeah?" Taking her unspoken lead, spouses held hands; others studied their cups.

A biting temptation urged Veen to warn the orphans of the war. They were the ones in danger. Nelis would've. "I should see to my brother," he said to Elanis before he rushed out the door.

Teallaigh Te mourned too often, drank and sang for the dead too many times. Veen didn't realize he was running until Elanis called after him. He didn't slow. He couldn't. Nelis needed to know about Tabbi. Veen needed to know his brother was safe. He hated to admit it, but Nelis wasn't as invincible as they all pretended.

Shuttered and locked, his home stirred his pulse. Veen pounded on the door twice before fishing out his key. Inside, embers roasted in the fireplace. He burst into Nelis's room. No Nelis. Veen leaped the bed and opened his ma's kast. No Heart.

"Veen," Elanis called from the other room.

"He's gone, El!"

"Calm yourself," Oren said at the doorway. "He left a note."

Veen joined him. As Elanis lifted a shred of old parchment from the table, he asked, "What's it say?"

Reading aloud, she held the parchment close to her spectacles. "I'm fine. Doing what needs doing." She dropped the yellowed sliver on the table and stabbed it with her finger a few times. "At least we know it's his. Laconic as ever when words are precious." Her grimace deepened as she thought.

Oren sank onto one of the ladder-back chairs and rubbed his temples. "Teague needs to know."

"Hey now," Veen said. "Maybe he's just hiding it? Maybe burying it somewhere safe?"

"He deceived us," Elanis said. "Wittingly."

"That makes him an arsehole, not a traitor!"

"Regardless," Oren said in a commanding tone, "our leader will know. We've been making his decisions since we got to this island."

The thought of telling Teague didn't soothe Veen's stomach any. "What's to stop Teague from going to Clarkson? If the Hook catches wind of what that relic may be able to do, they'll hunt Nelis." Oren flashed him a patronizing look. "Don't! Don't defend them! You know men and power. Even if Clarkson weren't Racinian, I'd not tempt him with that honey. Sorry, El."

The Racinian mage playfully punched him in the arm. "Trust in Teague, Little Nelis. Should Teague suggest the doubtful, we'll change his mind."

With mild agreement, they went to the Tulip and arranged a carriage to Aontus. The three mercenaries waited in silence and then in sparsely shared words after they'd begun their trek.

Finally, Veen couldn't stand it. "While you two tell Teague, I'll search the Tower, yeah? He might've gone after Mage Curtiss. Maybe we should check there first, just to be sure."

Oren looked back to the green field of spelt beside the road. "Teague first."

Elanis kicked Veen's foot with her dirty boot. "You're not forcing me into an onerous confession by myself."

Night had overtaken them when they arrived at the approach to the Fuchses' manor. Their timing as fortunate as ever, they disembarked to find Teague's parents eyeing them curiously. Dressed as Veen imagined merchants always dressed, a silver-haired man stood next to a gold-encrusted carriage. If the fire opals on the doors hadn't told Veen he was Teague's father, his stretched body and fox face would've. His mother, dignified and handsome, stopped Veen where he stood by her beauty alone. She lifted her hefty skirts to lean inside the carriage and say something. Teague's head popped out. Concerned, he ignored his father's calls and came straight to them.

"And there he is," Elanis said. "Teague as I first met him, lace collar and all."

"Aye," Teague said with a charming grin. "Cannot say I've missed it. So go on now. What possessed ye to enter this asp pit? Ye seem to have forgotten someone." Elanis and Veen looked to Oren. "Oh, there's the good man," Teague continued. "Just being cautious, I see. Cannot blame him for dragging his heavy heels when coming here."

Veen perked up at the familiar mountainy silhouette coming up the bricks from the road. Tired and cloaked, Nelis slowed his approach when he saw them. Over his shoulder, a slim leather satchel hung. Only missives came in those kinds of satchels.

"By the gods, you went to Racine?" Veen asked, hardly believing the words after they'd left his mouth.

Nelis answered, "Had to talk to Clarkson."

"About what, now?" Teague asked. His demeanor darkened when Nelis ignored the question.

The crotal bells of the horses chimed as they wheeled Lord and Lady Fuchs's carriage away without their son.

"New orders," Nelis said, handing over the satchel to Teague. "Need to strike off to the docks if youse're going to catch the last galleon to Trône d'Argent."

Teague's gloved fingers undid the silver chain running through the hook-and-sword emblem on the satchel's flap and removed a scroll from inside.

"I can't go to Racine like this," Elanis said, brushing her dirty legs down for good measure.

Teague moved closer to one of the lampposts lining the approach. Elanis read over his shoulder. Both skeptics eyed Nelis when they'd finished. Teague's cheeks grew dark. His mouth thinned to a line before he offered the scroll to Oren.

Elanis muttered, "No. I was mantled too recently."

Nelis tapped the parchment in Oren's fingers. "Clarkson's seal. Clarkson's missive. Can't argue with it."

"What?" Veen asked.

"I'm the new liaison between the Hook and the Tower of Trône d'Argent," she answered. Her face seemed too frightened to express joy, as though the joke would be revealed the second she believed it. "Grand Diviner Sylvester agreed?"

"I gave Clarkson something to make him listen, didn't I?"

"You let him have the Heart?" Elanis asked.

Veen scoffed before Elanis put an arm between him and his brother.

"The Heart?" Teague asked. "Rethfor's Heart?"

Nelis confirmed it with a guiltless nod. "Safer with the Hook than back in the temple. Youse three are off." He thumbed to the road behind him. "Clarkson says to deliver the empty chest to Mage Curtiss tomorrow. Runt and I will deal with what needs doing here."

Teague stepped up to Nelis, his fury visible in the inches between their faces. Nelis broke his gaze. "I deserve an explanation," Teague said.

"We'll catch up—"

"Oren, El, we're on the next boat," Teague interrupted. "I have three empty spots in my band to fill before we report to the bloody hills of Delpharn."

Nelis raised his hands to pacify Teague. "No, you have one to fill. Veen and I will catch up to youse there within the week."

Teague snatched the scroll from Oren and smashed it against Nelis's chest. "You assume you're welcome. Guard duty for a baron's daughter in the Warring States? Did you choose that simpleton assignment for us?"

Nelis's lips barely moved when he replied. "You're down a few; they keep saying that's bad luck, making it true. I needed to know you'd be safe."

"Right," Teague said coolly. "How could you make a decision like that without consulting me?" He pointed for the others to get in their coach. Gesturing to her muddy clothes, Elanis silently protested. "We'll change in the docks on the other side, El. Veen, you're welcome to find us, if you want. But you, Nelis, you can keep your counsel and your secrets."

Teague crumpled the letter in his fist and stalked off, complaining about buying new clothes in Racine. Without further explanation, Veen's band loaded into the coach from Teallaigh Te and rode on, leaving him behind with the traitor in the wet night.

Fuming, Nelis fogged the air with his nostrils and wandered to stand alone. Veen left him while the minutes passed, not sure he could speak to him right then. Nelis groaned a few times and huffed. He shook his head, then shook his arms. Tight-lipped, he gave a furious nod and abruptly darted after the carriage.

Veen kept pace. They dashed through every shortcut he knew to get to the wharf. Finally, at the end of the butter slip to the old market, they padded along the planks of the wharf. Before a gull-covered statue of Wee Will, the one merchant who had turned his back on Racine in the revolution and had been consequently drawn and quartered by his associates, a couple of porters unloaded Elanis's possessions.

Nelis dodged through the crowd and grabbed Teague's forearm. In an overpowering tug, Nelis brought Teague against him. He planted a kiss on Teague's lips, gentle and welcomed by their leader. Veen's body tensed.

Elanis and Oren smirked before the mage made her way through the lurking onlookers to Veen. She hugged him farewell, though he hardly noticed beyond the floral scent growing fainter to let the tanning yard's stink back in.

A filthy beggar barked laughs and insults from the crowd observing the kissing mercenaries. Nelis ran his knuckles down Teague's cheek and whispered. They parted with longing glances, Teague's still wounded.

While his band boarded a Racinian galleon and floated out to sea, Veen pieced together the furtive snickers and inside jokes he'd misunderstood. A loud splash summoned his attention back to the docks. Crying for help, the whooping beggar floundered in the water. Nelis threw a rude gesture to the splashing man before he dragged Veen through the gawking crowd, back to the butter slip.

Halfway through the old market to New Market, Nelis took an unexpected turn. Bounding down a ditch, he made sure no one could see them. Then he pulled open an iron-bar grate leading to the sewers. "I can tell by your sour face you want answers. Get in."

"Away and fuck yourself, Nelis," Veen growled. "I don't know who you are. Show me this bastard mage who has addled my brother's mind so badly he's stolen the Heart from the lowlanders forever."

"Oh, you'll see the bastard all right," Nelis said, climbing inside. "And before you start yelling about the Heart, meet our true benefactor. You and Elanis . . . youse may have done us a grand favor."

Veen took a regretful inhale and clanged the sewer gate in place behind them.

"Just you wait, Runt. After you learn the truth, even you'd be tempted to hand it over."

Chapter 9: The van Veen Boys

The sewers granted Veen and Nelis passage to the necropolis spanning the underside of Aontus. Squat oil lamps had been placed by the Wives where each stone arc touched the ground, interrupting the stacked bones. These crypt-filled tunnels differed from those occupying Mount Noafa by delving into prehistory. With their twisting, rising, and falling at the whims of the ancients, these tunnels had Nelis grunting in annoyance before they'd gone a quarter of a mile.

Veen's nerves cooled some during the dank walk. "You could have told me. About you and Teague."

"You could have figured it out. We weren't good at hiding it, no? Teague didn't want to."

"Why did you?"

"You're not dumb enough to ask that," his brother snapped.

Allowing Nelis a long lead, Veen stared daggers hotter than that blazing short sword. Nelis picked up his pace, probably feeling Veen's eyes on him and taking it for a specter. But then, he, too, felt more than the skulls watching them.

Another door of iron bars separated the lit passages from the truly ancient depths not tended to by the Wives. Nelis's short sword gave off enough light to keep them from tripping over their toes.

They rounded a corner into a passage Veen would have missed through the shadows. When Nelis's blade rose before him, orange light glinted up the rods of a rusted gate.

"The other night," Nelis whispered as he opened the gate, "while you and Elanis were pleasing the fairies at the Boyd Estate, I went back to the Tower. Had some questions for the paralibrarian about what I saw in Dreanen's study." He shook his head. "I'll tell you later. Anyroads, Dreanen himself skulked out all determined, yeah? So I tailed him. Down here."

Damp stone passages stinking of mold reminded Veen of the final challenge in the Hook's labyrinth, strengthening his discomfort. It had taken the six of them to survive it, even if Veen had been the one to deliver the final blow to the "minotaur," a fury. His first kill. The crazed magus had threatened anyone and everyone. Still, Veen carried the deed with him. Like a scratch on his gums, it refused to go numb. Recalling the peace entering the man's eyes helped some.

Something fuzzy and white covered the walls where they made a right turn. Eventually, lamplight washed down the tunnel. Nelis sheathed his blade and tiptoed until his hand told Veen to stop. "We'll be a powerful surprise but shouldn't be in danger. I think." He checked Veen to make sure he had his daggers. Veen brushed him off. They sneaked forward.

At the tunnel's end, two men spoke lowly as they argued over papers spread out on an old altar. Round and domed, the chamber dipped slightly toward the altar in its middle. Fire roiled in the fireplace behind the men. Standing proudly in his amber mantle, Mage Curtiss stretched a foot taller than the man wearing lowlander armor, simple splint mail reinforced with wood. Was it a rule that you had to wear green robes if you were mantled in the old Amber and Green?

Nelis sauntered out of the shadows and dropped heavy footsteps. The lowlander soldier drew his dagger and rushed to meet him.

Veen ran forward and separated from Nelis to challenge the lanky mage if things weren't as peaceful as Nelis had predicted. Despite his beard, this Mage Curtiss couldn't have been much older than Veen. No wonder Nelis kept calling him Dreanen. Long brown hair touched the mage's shoulder when his head cocked to exude irritation. Unlike Elanis, he wore his component pouches tucked under his belt, rendering him easily disarmed.

The deep velvet sack hanging over the mage's right hip held Veen's attention until Nelis said, "Da." A chill gripped Veen's legs.

"Nelis?" the armored man asked. His voice did sound familiar. Midway between Veen's and Nelis's heights, the man had less hair than Nelis, but shared their nose. He sheathed his dagger. "And Little Stille? What are youse boys doing here?" the ghost scolded.

Veen's voice cracked when he asked, "And Ma?"

The older Stille van Veen took a deep breath and shook his head. "No. She's the true martyr of Teallaigh Te, so she is." He drifted behind his eyes as he came to Veen.

"How?" Veen asked. "How did it happen?"

"Don't summon that dark night, son." His da swallowed and rested his warm hands on Veen's shoulders. "You have Iona's eyes. Melts my heart to see those again. And her ears." He laughed and hugged him. "Cherish the hair while you've got it, boy." The memories Veen held on to of his father were few and far between, mostly fleeting moments when he'd managed to gain his attention. But he smelled the same. Pipe smoke and peat with a bit of a hard day's work. "On her dying breath, your ma made me swear to keep youse away from the rebellion. Don't fault me for honoring her wish."

His father reached for Nelis, but his brother brushed past him to examine what lay on the altar. "Do us a favor, then," Nelis said. The anger in his voice jarred Veen; his brain still spun out questions, disbelieving his senses. But then, Nelis had known their father lived. "Reveal another of your secrets, yeah? Why do you need the Heart of Rethfor?"

"Ye weren't supposed to open the chest," Mage Curtiss said with a quiet fury. From his pinned scarf to the lace-cut leather overlaying his belt, it was obvious that the mage had wealth. His hand clutched a bumpy mulberry-purple tome on the altar and swung it up under his armpit. Leathery thorns of dark skin covered the surface. "Where is it now?"

"Safe," Nelis answered.

"We need that relic!" the mage yelled. "Without it, we cannot save them."

"Who?" Nelis asked.

"Hold," their da said. "Let me talk to my sons, Dreanen."

The mage didn't budge.

"Youse weren't supposed to steal the chest until tomorrow night, boys. Dreanen would've explained it all then."

"You knew?" Veen blurted.

The mage gave a barely audible grunt. Veen's father fixed a scowl on Dreanen. "Give us some time, boy. My sons have had a serious shock."

Panting through his nostrils, Dreanen stood his ground. "Fix this, Stille. They'll ruin everything."

"Have youse heard of the Filii Cinere?" his da asked.

Veen let Nelis answer with a shake of his head.

"A sect of rich feckers who want to restore Merith's ways to the continent. They all but rule the merchants and the nobles. True to Merith, they're trying to do so on someone else's back. Youse have heard our people are being abducted?"

"Of course we have," Nelis answered. "Are you saying they've been taken by these slavers?"

"Sure as there's warm blood in my veins. Slaves. Did youse see any while nosing about the Boyd Estate?"

"No," Veen answered. "Hardly anyone at all."

"No matter," Dreanen said. "I need to continue our preparations." Covering the tome with his mantle, he frowned at Nelis. "Bring the Heart to the new temple tomorrow night, as ye've already committed to doing, mercenaries. Climb the scaffolding in the southwest corner and find me in the Wives' prayer room. If ye arrive after the Glades have reached their apex, ye'll be too late to help our kin." Disappearing into the tunnel, Dreanen left them with the ghost and the freedom to ask some questions.

"Our kin?" Veen asked. "Da, who is that Dreanen fella?"

"Didn't expect to catch me gabbing with the upper sort?" his da asked.

"I didn't expect any of this. But, aye, that's odd."

"Bah, Dreanen's the right sort. Former ward of Wee Will himself." He cleared his throat. "Youse shouldn't be here, boys. 'Tisn't what your ma wanted."

"You hired our band," Nelis said bitterly. "Perhaps you would have kept your promise if you hadn't done that."

"Aye," their da said. "I admit I wanted you boys to be a part of this. 'Tis in your blood, in your heritage. But not this deep."

"No changing it now," Nelis replied.

"Suppose, suppose." His father patted Veen's shoulder. "Iona'll be sharpening her words for me, but good to have youse with us."

"Why are you hiding?" Veen asked. "The war is over."

His father retracted his arm. "The Filii Cinere. Racine. The Bo'Anboes. Merith before all of them." He went to stand by Nelis, who shuffled through maps on the altar. Their da picked up a handful of parchment, beat it against his palm, and threw it onto the altar. "Our enemies are related. They're different, sure, but their blood won't stop hounding our people. The war against the lowlanders continues whether youse see it or not, Little Stille."

Nelis cleared the papers his father had thrown from the map he'd been studying. "You've not told us how the Heart is going to help you."

"Help us," his da corrected. "'Twill help us, son. Dreanen doesn't tell me the whos and whats of it; I'm not a mage, yeah? Have a little faith and help us bring the enslaved home."

"Stille," Dreanen called. Veen jumped when the man appeared behind him. "Maso a anthu ambiri," he breathed and tossed a packet onto the fireplace. A flash of blue light erupted from the flames. "I require your assistance. Alone."

"Right," Nelis said. He rounded the opposite side of the altar from the mage and took Veen by the arm. "Time for my brother and I to have ourselves a wee talk."

"Nelis," his father called. "You want to find Dundy? To find Tabbira? We'll need the Heart."

"How did you know about Tabbi?" Nelis asked.

"The dead hear all sorts of tales, son."

"Don't call me that!" Nelis blustered. "You weren't there. For any of us!"

His da's shoulders went back. "You think the peace you've been enjoying just happened on its own?"

"Regardless," Dreanen cut in, "there is no other way to save them. Their fate is tied to the Heart. Without it, they are surely dead."

"Dead?" Veen asked.

"Would you not choose death over slavery?" his da asked disappointedly. "Lowlanders don't surrender."

Nelis tightened his grip on Veen's arm and pulled him along. "Then we'll see youse at the temple."

Dragged along like a child, Veen jerked against his brother's hold to no avail. He punched Nelis in the gut. Nelis didn't respond. In the lantern-lit necropolis, he did it again. Nelis wasn't there, lost in his head. Veen lowered his voice, which took the force out of it, but said, "What if Da knew you warmed the sheets with a merchant's son?"

Nelis spun around and pinned Veen against the bones. His face invaded Veen's vision. His nostrils blew hot air. "Your gob had better never bring Teague into this." Two seconds of scowling and he released him.

He didn't respond to Veen again until they stood in the middle of the Jervis Bridge. Now and then, lightning from the northern clouds lit the sky well enough to see the Tower and its spinning sails. "You get it now?" Nelis asked. "Some resistance they are. Two men."

"Could be four."

"Maybe there already are," Nelis said. "Maybe himself is behind the Five Snakes escape. 'Twould explain why they had a map of the prison." He leaned back against the filigree railing and crossed his arms, then his legs. "What did you see in there, Runt?"

"Our dead da for one! Nelis, tell me you didn't know."

"No," Nelis said. "Not before that night. And when I saw him, I swear to Rethfor, I thought he was a ghost. But ghosts don't have foggy breath, yeah?" He studied the sky. "Then I started wondering why. If he's been alive all of these years, why didn't he tell us? Why hasn't he been there for us?"

"Nelis," Veen moaned with sudden realization. "El and I can vouch for the Filii Cinere being here. The vault—gods, the entire Boyd Estate—glorified Merith. Statues, armor, shields, even a bloody speaker's collar. If they're trying to enslave the magi again, I can see why Dreanen would be an arse about it."

Thunder suggested they find shelter soon. Veen bent over the side of the bridge to view the smooth river passing under them. "Da is alive. We should be—"

"Did you see the book?" Nelis asked, adopting that patient-father stare of his. "Dreanen's?"

"The purple one? Yeah, what of it?"

"That's varrow hide, Runt."

Drenching the word in skepticism, Veen repeated, "Varrow? Away with you, Nelis." He was having him on. There wasn't a magus alive who'd risk tempting one of those fiends from the shadows.

"Verified it at the Tower myself. The mage in the arcanum said the only reason to bind a tome in that skin is to conceal the contents from scrying. Something about the oils."

"That only means Dreanen's got his secrets. If they're breaking into prisons, it seems smart, so."

Feigning bucked teeth, Nelis mocked the paralibrarian who had assisted him, "'The only true way to tempt a varrow is with a corpse that has tasted death thrice.'" He studied the Tower. "That's when I knew we'd stepped in it. I tried to blame my questions on a dream, which made it worse. Feckin' mages and their tireless tongues.

"That boyo, Dreanen, is a necromancer. You see why I had to get the others away from this hash? No Racinian. No merchant's son. No Caperi."

Nodding his understanding, Veen imagined Oren's reaction to a mage crossing that line. Necromancy had driven his people from their islands and into the ocean, right into more hardships awaiting them on the continent. Dreanen would have lost his head before the introductions had ended, assuming Oren knew what the tome meant.

But they were talking about their father's friend. "Ach! Nelis, he probably nicked the tome from a Tower."

The buckteeth returned. "'None are known to exist. Varrows are unwelcome in any form in this world.'"

Veen's thoughts grew heavy, allowing the sensibility he'd been swatting away to swarm. "Then," he uttered, "what is he up to?"

Nelis tapped his nose. "Good man. Now what do you say we get the Heart from where I hid it and solve this puzzle as members of the Hook rather than blindly following Da's lead?"

Chapter IO: Ceremony of Corpses

Shrugging off his opinion of the shield Nelis had picked up from the merchant's table, Veen quietly asked, "So without the Heart, how'd you bribe Clarkson to appoint Elanis as liaison?" He felt foolish whispering; no one paid them any mind in the morning bustle of New Market, but nothing felt certain after the events of last night.

Nelis shifted and sighed. "Let's just say I won't be expecting payment for a few years."

"Years?" Veen squawked, gaining the attention of the merchant's helper.

"'Tisn't too old, I assure youse—ye," the aide said. After the commoner slip of the tongue, he adjusted the plush flat cap on his head, which he'd donned backward with the feather falling in front of his face. "Just as old as the war."

"I know," Nelis said, putting his right arm through the straps. The round brass shield guarded his arm to just above his elbow. He let the light play over the surface's designs. "Bog orchids and hearts for Rethfor. How'd your master come by it? Fought against Racine, did he?"

Sensing the crudely concealed trap in Nelis's words, the merchant's helper smacked his lips, then thought with his mouth open. When the oars stopped rowing behind his eyes, he bent across the table and practically breathed, "I can't take less than three silvers."

Nelis glanced over to Veen and inclined his head toward the aide. Smirking at Veen's frown, Nelis said, "Consider it your turn, brother."

"You take Frysta Avfall coin?" Veen asked.

"Aye—yes," the aide said, relieved by Nelis's grin. "If ye'll come to the scales."

Trade completed, they ventured south to the inn room they'd secured under the Hook's standard barter, double the cost for the delay in direct payment from the guild's coffers. Nelis removed his gambeson and collapsed across his bed.

"Should we see if we've gotten a nibble yet?" Veen asked. They needed information, and when it came to the Filii Cinere, there was a serious lack of it to be found.

Burying his face in his pillow, Nelis said, "Get some rest. It has only been hours since we offered the reward. Half of our Aunt Sheryls are just waking up. Let them get their tea and spread the word a bit."

"You rest. I'm going downstairs for a cha myself."

"That reminds me." Nelis dug around in his pocket and held his fist out. Veen put his hand under it. "You left these at the hall the other night." Five dice landed in his palm.

"Ah, thanks very much." He rattled the dice in his hand as he went to play the card up his sleeve. After checking with the innkeeper for messages and discovering Nelis had been correct, he made his way to the messenger stalls near the port.

"Where to?" a spritely girl with a long flaxen braid asked.

Her inviting eyes made him fumble his words, but he managed, "Teallaigh Te," on his third attempt. Using the last of the coin in his pockets, he paid for urgency. She handed him parchment and directed him to the writing desks. Flushed and wishing he'd bathed before coming, he didn't look her way until he'd sealed the letter to Gbad'Wu.

The Ukresti of the Mount may not teach the same abilities as the spellbreaker monasteries, but his gut told him to seek any help he could. Gods, he may already be too late. Assuring himself that Gbad'Wu would want to know the connection to the missing villagers regardless, he handed the message to the girl and scampered back to the inn.

The afternoon passed without a bite on the reward offered for information. Nelis joined him for a light dinner of beef-and-cabbage stew. Too much food was a recipe for dull wits and slow reflexes, the likes of which his sharpened daggers couldn't overcome. When the Tower's younglings began lighting the lanterns throughout the old market, Veen said, "A reward of ten gold and we didn't even get a decent lie? I'm not sure I know our kin at all anymore."

"Speaks a mouthful," Nelis said. He drummed his thick fingers on the table. "In Da's favor. Either this cult of yours is so far removed from our folk they know nothing of it, or they're too afraid to speak against it."

He stood and hefted the shield that had been leaning against his chair. "We did what we could. Time to do what we must."

The fickle rain had cleared away, leaving the evening crisp and starry. The visible half of the pale moon had more than a few hours to ascend before they were late. Worming through the town's many estates, they avoided guards for sport on their way toward Teague's family estate. The Fuchses' gardens were bountiful, vast, and thoroughly vacant.

"You didn't honestly think I'd tell Da about Teague?" Veen asked.

Nelis grunted. "He's not the lenient sort, Runt. The war forged a zealot's heart in his chest long before his 'death.'" He walked backward down an aisle flanked by rosy hydrangeas. "Himself has been here all that time and never offered us a feather. 'The war against the lowlanders continues whether youse see it or not.' Arsehole. He's probably only bothered by the Filii Cinere because they're taking his soldiers."

"Poor Dundy," Veen muttered.

Nelis waved off the topic.

"What I'm saying is I'm sorry," Veen said. "Tattling wouldn't be my first inclination upon seeing Da back from the dead." Veen stopped. "He's not actually back from the dead, no?"

Nelis pondered the question before he answered, "Don't be an eejit. How many times has Oren said they come back mindless, like wights in the old tales?"

At the end of the hydrangeas, stairs led down to an open-air temple devoted to Maris, the goddess of companionship.

Nelis nudged him. "Thanks." Veen didn't understand his meaning until he had already made for the narrow flight of steps. Down they crept.

Modest for a merchant construct, the temple provided benches in alcoves hidden behind rosebushes along the outer edge. Delicate hands had molded the ten-foot marble idol of Maris. Alabaster robes draped under one of her breasts, round with a daringly pointed nipple. A softly chiseled smirk teased Veen while he took it in. "I see why Teague favors Maris."

"Shut it, Runt."

Nelis rounded the idol's pedestal, which was shrouded in heart-shaped ivy. Bricks clinked as he pulled them from the base and stacked them aside. He reached in and removed a satchel. Veen took it. Warm to the touch. He lashed it around his chest and tightened it against him. "How did you know to hide it there?"

"You'd hear it; then you'd want to disremember it," Nelis answered. Taking him at his word, Veen let it go. Nelis twisted his lips as he inspected Maris. "Let's not wait around for more trouble."

"Hold on, Nelis. We have hours still." And he needed to give his message to Gbad'Wu time to do any good. "Do you think Da is responsible for the merchants' burned warehouses on the docks all those years back and the murdered Racinians in Keane Square two years ago?"

"And the Albacore?" Nelis asked. "I don't know. We'll ask himself when this is over. Just remember, Runt, we don't owe him a feckin' thing."

Heading south, they stuck to the woods edging the estates until they reached the temple grounds. With their hoods up, people wearing gray cloaks trickled from the main road and through the doors whose braziers had not been lit. The cloaks kept coming. Eventually, only stragglers sped inside.

There was no sign of Gbad'Wu, even atop the scaffolding. His message must not have arrived in time. Or perhaps she wasn't in Teallaigh Te any longer.

Nelis struck off. His shield dimly reflected the moonlight as he dashed toward the scaffolding. They ascended to the empty window in the southwest corner and entered.

The square prayer room nurtured its shadows. Tightly arranged pews faced a small unlit brazier. A figure watched them from the open edge of the room, where a black marble handrail and stone balusters guarded against a misstep and fall to the sanctuary below. Firelight danced along the underside of the buttresses behind Dreanen. The mage put a finger to his lips and gestured them forward.

In the sanctuary below, the Filii Cinere sat motionless in the pews. Their gray masks watched the elevated hearth. Inside the hearth's brazier, two women and three men struggled against their bindings.

"Slaves," Nelis uttered.

Yes, Veen could barely make out the Vetskarran brandings on their cheeks. But they weren't the missing lowlanders.

The mage's eyes wandered over them. "Did you bring it?"

Nelis nodded.

A broad-chested man held his hood high and ascended the steps to the slaves. At the top, he raised a curved dagger for the audience to see and held the blade before the nose of his mask. Silently, the Filii Cinere stood and placed their right hands on themselves. Some grasped their throats. Some covered their hearts, while others were more suggestive. The dagger pointed to a Filii Cinere grabbing her other hand.

Dreanen returned to the prayer room and untucked a small pouch from his belt. He unbound the mouth of it and lowered it inside the brazier. "Ignolio fervente." Fire swept over the dried peat, shining upon the underside of the mage's face. Mirrors and glass spread the light to the amber tulips and red jasper harts inset along the walls.

Reaching to the slaves, the Filii Cinere on the hearth grabbed a woman's arm and pulled her close. She cried out but didn't seem to know which way to dodge. He raised her arm out before he raised his blade.

"Save them!" Nelis said.

Dreanen warmed his bony fingers over the fire. "I cannot."

"You're a mage; you can do something!"

Another pouch came out from behind Dreanen's belt. "No, I cannot. They're already gone. See the way they jerk away from the very air itself? Poisonous hallucinations. Those masked cowards wouldn't risk facing their inferiors without assurances." The slave screamed.

Dreanen sighed. "Uneducated filth. They believe the temple can be desecrated to an extent the consecration won't take root next week; the prayers to Rethfor will die on the floor and extend his absence. Afraid the gods will stop their new Merith. But they truly know no gods to fear beyond society. Break their masks and see how bold they are." He locked eyes with Nelis and held out his hand. "We must end them. The stone?"

"The Heart," Nelis corrected.

"What'll you do with it?" Veen asked.

"A holy sacrifice."

Nelis placed his hand on the hilt of his short sword. "What's this got to do with the missing lowlanders? Were they sacrificed?"

Dreanen fixed his stare on Veen and hummed a noncommittal response. "Nothing has happened to them that cannot be undone. With the Heart."

Veen backed away from the wild-eyed mage and repositioned the warm satchel to rest on his lower back.

The mage drew a dagger from his sleeve and sliced the back side of his forearm. "Ye wish to save your friends? Then permit me a more direct explanation." The bloody blade plunged into the burning peat. Clenching his hand before his face, Dreanen said, "Come."

A squeak brought Veen's attention back to the sanctuary. The Filii Cinere didn't take their eyes from the butchering to see Stille van Veen, dressed in his lowlander splint mail, propping open the temple's doors. He left. Other armored men shuffled inside and clogged the exit.

When the lowlander men reached the middle of the pews, a gray-masked woman screamed. She scrambled over the pews away from the lowlander soldiers. The man next to her wasn't as fast. The nimbler lowlanders wrestled down the Filii Cinere and bit him through his clothes. Savagely, mindlessly, they tore his flesh.

Wights. Shroud-eaters.

Filii Cinere broke their silence as they ran to huddle behind the temple's hearth. More undead emerged from the stairs to the catacombs, scattering the gray cloaks. Lowlander commoners. More than a dozen. Veen counted twenty-five, no, thirty.

"What is this?" Veen asked over the startled shouts.

"A solution," Dreanen answered. "Warriors marching under our banner without fear, without doubt. When they are finished, I will use the Heart to restore their lives."

The enchanted blade in Nelis's left hand glowed.

"I sense your disapproval. Can ye truly sympathize with these bigots?"

Below, the wights lurched forward whenever one of the Filii Cinere ventured too close. They snatched one. The man lost his mask as he fought back. Veen recognized him from the estate. The old man with the map. His struggling knocked the helmet off a round head of shockingly ginger hair. "Dundy," Veen said. Dundy tore the man's gut open.

Nelis raised his shield toward the mage. "Where'd Da go?"

Dreanen casually answered, "To thin the herd."

"Meaning?"

"The Filii Cinere span generations. The adults are here." The mage smirked.

"Where?" Nelis demanded.

"Give me the Heart!" Dreanen spit. He withdrew from the brazier and opened the only door to the prayer room. "'Tis the only way to save your friends now. Including, of course, Tabbira." Upon mention of the name, Tabbi's body shuffled through the doorway, still dressed in a Wife's robes. Matted with mud and leaves, her raven hair clung to the skin around her unseeing eyes. Nelis's sword broiled the air and brightened to white.

A weak moan preceded three decaying arms hooking over the marble rail. Veen drew his daggers. Nelis hauled him back. "Heart or head. If they have their flesh, heart or head," Nelis whispered, repeating Oren's advice. Dundy and an unrecognizable woman climbed over the railing and hobbled to their summoner's side. Rot revealed spots of grayed meat through their skin, though Dundy had fewer than his companion.

The heat of the blade held them back as Nelis pressed Veen through the pews and toward the window to the scaffolding. "Dundy, Tabbi, forgive us; we're not doing it. You could turn us all into those things."

"Ye know the truth of the relics?" Dreanen asked. "Aye, I could turn Aontus into an unquestioning army to march against Racine. Or I will do as I have promised your father I would do, and cure them. I bear no ill will toward our brethren, even the cowards who refused to fight at our side. With a relic, I can compel their souls to return from the Glades."

Every muscle in Nelis's face tensed as he shook his head.

"I will save them. But they must save us first."

Through the window, a young man's body followed his stench inside. Skitter O'Hallorhan—or what was left of him. Gods, he hardly resembled the boy who had always split his pies over a game of knucklebones at the docks.

An unrecognizable bloat behind Skitter slipped on its own peeling skin and toppled onto the windowsill with a squish.

"Never," Nelis said.

Dreanen asked, "Why not consult Tabbira first? Speak, Wife."

Tabbira's jaw worked, but her voice failed to manifest above a rattle.

Dreanen examined the wight. "She's supposed to be pleading for your help. No bother." The mage wrapped his scarf around his hand and stuck it into the brazier. His dagger arched up, into Tabbi's heart. Her corpse toppled backward to the floor.

Nelis's roar was drowned by a birdlike screech emanating from the shadows of the opened door. A leathery purple tail whipped into the light, spearing Tabbi's chest with the arced black bone at its end. Her body jerked into the shadows.

"Third time's the charm," Dreanen said.

"What kind of madman smiles after summoning a fecking varrow?" Veen asked.

Nelis drove his blade through Skitter's skull. Then he hoisted his shield up under Skitter's ribs and shoved the corpse and the bloated wight with enough force to clear the platform outside. "Go, Runt!"

But the opening didn't last. Veen had no sooner swung his leg over the sill than three more wights climbed up the scaffolding to take Skitter's place.

While Nelis fed the wights his blade and knocked them back to the scaffolding, Veen put his back and the Heart to the corner. The bodies clogged the entry, allowing only the most determined to dig their way through. Veen looked to Nelis for their plan. If varrows were like basilisks, or most magical beasties, only Nelis's weapon had any hope of penetrating its hide.

"Stop eating and get in here!" Dreanen yelled to the dark corridor.

A jagged black spike on the varrow's horned-toad-like head moved into the light. The form of a spiky panther followed. Aiming his brow spike at Dreanen, the varrow warned him with a rattling hiss. Dreanen flinched and pointed at Veen. All six of the varrow's yellow eyes snapped to Veen before the spike lowered at him.

Nelis edged away from the window. The beast slung its tail spike but struck the shield and punctured a pew, which trapped the bone in dense wood. Nelis rushed down the central aisle and smacked the varrow with his shield. The blow knocked its head aside. But before he could drive his sword into its throat, Dundy slammed into him.

"This is not a dilemma you find yourself in, Little Stille," Dreanen said. "You have one option. Surrender and I'll return the varrow to the shadows."

Another wight broke through the pile at the window. Mercifully, the struggling purple tail caught his attention and drew him close. His bite sent the varrow into a hissing frenzy. The arced blade dislodged from the pew and sliced cleanly through the wight's shoulder and head.

While the varrow sniffed its tail, Veen dived between the pews and started crawling toward Nelis. His brother shoved against Dundy's crushing weight. The wight's drool dripped from the edge of Nelis's shield. His short sword lay five feet out of his reach, beneath the pews in the front row. Nelis's eyes went to it, then to Veen.

The varrow screeched. It leaped onto the pews where Veen had been. The beast's talons scraped along the wood for a grip, but toppled them. Veen crawled faster. He was almost there.

The varrow's tail spike stabbed through the pew ahead of him, chipping into the tile floor. An unnatural chatter rattled above him. Talons ripped across his back. Veen screamed. His skin burned.

"Runt!" Nelis yelled. He threw Dundy back and caught him with his heels. The wight swiped again. Nelis kicked against Dundy, propelling himself forward, and grabbed his sword. The brass handle clinked as it slid across the tiles, straight to Veen. Releasing his dagger, Veen snatched the sword.

Dundy fell flat on Nelis and sank his teeth into his right sleeve. "No!" Veen yelled.

Veen rolled onto his aching back. The varrow's fetid breath panted down on him as its six eyes studied his face. It bared its black teeth and lunged. Veen got the heated blade between them. The full weight of the varrow knocked the sword out of his grasp, driving the pommel into the tile next to Veen's head. Limp, the beast's body fell to the pew with the blade encased in its skull.

Veen scrambled up and groaned as he wrenched the sword free. Dundy stood motionless behind Dreanen. A small pouch rested open in the mage's hand.

Nelis dangled, pinned to the wall by a spell. Blood ran down his right hand from his stained sleeve. "Nelis!" Veen called. His brother didn't rouse.

"He lives," Dreanen said. "I had promised your father not to harm ye. You see, I respect the man. He taught me how dark the world truly is, to see where the true threats lie." Dreanen pointed toward the sanctuary. His hands joined behind his back. "But no one wants to fight anymore. Too complacent to dirty their hands. So I took away their choice. And ye're making it far more tempting to count ye in their numbers than ye should. Now, Little Stille, you've slain a varrow. Be the hero and save your brother, too."

The blade in Veen's hand hissed when it came too close to a pew and scorched the wood. "Our ma died to keep this Heart—"

Dreanen's pouch hit the floor under Nelis and spilled green sand. "It takes more than a bite to turn someone into a wight, you know? Oh, he'll have a fever for a day or two and will feel sluggish for a week, but he could recover." With his ring finger tucked into his palm, Dreanen waved his hand. "Kadav sèvi." Brilliant green fog crept out of the sand. "To become a wight, that needs to reach the wound. Act fast, Little Stille, while I can stop it."

Tendrils of the hex cracked loudly. Veen started. The fog crackled and brightened as it grew, then cracked again when it changed direction to coil up Nelis's boots. Tabbi hadn't been lying.

Nelis's dark eyes were open. They threatened a beating Veen might never recover from. The greater good. Veen's chest hurt, but he did as he was told. "You heard my brother, Dreanen. Never."

Dreanen threw his hands up. Labored breathing sounded behind Veen. The female wight that had climbed up with Dundy jumped onto his back. Drool dripped onto Veen's ear. He tried to shake her off. She moaned and dug her nails into his skin. Veen pressed the blade against her forearm and burned the decaying flesh.

Dundy dived onto the pair, smashing them against the pews. The impact disarmed Veen. Bones cracked. Only certain his dagger had lodged into Dundy, Veen writhed to reach the floor. His ankle remained pinned under Dundy's girth. Searching for a weapon, he spotted Dreanen's smirk at the end of the row.

Still drooling, Dundy hefted Veen off the floor. Veen kicked against the pews and wedged his shoulder under Dundy's meaty neck. He wasn't strong enough to budge him. His hands searched for his dagger along Dundy's belly. Hugged tightly against his old friend's body, Veen shouted as the mage stole the Heart from his satchel.

Blue tinged Nelis's lips. The fog was gone. Veen expected anger in his brother's eyes, but they were too glossy to hold emotion. "Save him!" Veen shouted.

Dreanen played his hand over the Heart. "No. Your father understands sacrifice." He slid the relic into his velvet sack. "On any scale."

"You said you'd save them. Save him now!" Veen yelled again as the mage passed his brother. He pressed against Dundy's hug with all his might. The spell suspending Nelis ended and dropped him to the floor.

Dreanen reappeared from the dark corridor. "Waste a weapon like this on cowards who won't raise a sword at their enemies? How quickly they forgot who wronged them. Not me!" He kicked Nelis's foot. "Besides, I prefer them the way they are." Dreanen shouted, "Eat, my soldiers! Let our foes know we'll clean their bones!"

The female wight rose. Her right arm flailed limply beneath protruding bone. His dagger was sheathed in her ribs. She rushed at him. Veen gripped the dagger and drove his knee into her chin. The blow hardly stalled her. His back flared in pain.

Ignoring it by focusing on Nelis, he shoved against the wight's chest with both of his knees. The dagger tore out. He jammed the blade upward into the fountain spilling its cold spit. They'd been friends once. But there was no saving Dundy, not without the Heart. Not with the Heart.

Freed, he slew the woman with a jab through her open mouth. Veen reached down to collect Nelis's sword before running to his brother.

Rolling Nelis over, Veen sputtered a prayer under his breath. His brother's skin had grown sallow in patches. Cold sweat had overtaken his face. But recognition returned to his eyes. "Don't talk, Nelis! Breathe!"

His eyes held that Nelis look. Certainty and a promise his fingers would warm tomorrow when they both had full bellies. The tenderness rarely uncaged. A slow smile reached his brother's lips.

"No," Nelis croaked. "Get. The Heart." Struggling to raise his left hand, Nelis moaned. He grabbed Veen's wrist and pleaded, "Avenge . . ." Tears beaded around his eyes as he put Veen's hand on the hilt of his short sword. Then he tapped the gambeson over his heart.

"Tell Teague—"

"He knows, Nelis." The comment actually brought some color to Nelis's cheeks.

With a long blink, Nelis said, "Now, Runt." His fingers fell.

"Nelis?" His breathing stopped. "Nelis?" Veen whined again. Trembling, Veen unlaced his brother's gambeson. He pulled the padding to the side and pointed the cold point of the blade at his brother's heart. There'd be no forgiveness for this. Disconnecting himself from any sensation, Veen closed his leaking eyes and put his weight against the hilt.

He quickly removed the sword and wiped at his face.

"Yes, eat their wicked marrow!" Dreanen's voice rang out from the sanctuary, interrupting Veen's sniffling. "Feast for our victory!"

Taking up his brother's sword, Veen ran to the railing. Dreanen's mantle shimmered before it disappeared through the entrance. The doors closed behind him.

Veen tasted the medallion on his tongue and leaped. He blew, gliding down to the sanctuary's back aisles. Misjudging the drop, he ran out of breath too soon. His groin absorbed the impact. The wights were too busy in their frenzied feasting to notice him before he hauled the right door open.

Focused solely on the mage, he hobbled as quickly as his body allowed. Then he sprinted. Dreanen had reached the trees at the edge of the temple grounds. No forgiveness.

Chapter II: Dark Magics

Veen roared a bestial yell when he tore through the trees lining the edge of the temple grounds. Dreanen couldn't outrun him on the grassy lawn. The mage's mantle shone in the moonlight.

With a smirk, the mage stopped and flung a stick behind him. "Apolithó méso!" The stick flared and crumbled. Veen slammed into nothing. He fell back, smelling the blood gushing from his nose before his hand wiped it from his lips. The air fell in on him, pinning him down.

"My da will put you down, Dreanen!"

Closing the space between them, Dreanen said, "Your father is a soldier, Little Stille." He pulled out the dagger he'd used on Tabbi. "As I said, he understands sacrifice. Probode." The blade twirled up to stand on its tip in the center of Dreanen's palm. It sliced down. Dreanen cried out before he refocused on Veen. Wincing, he slid the dagger free as he muttered, "Gradat vo ostrinata."

White light leaked from the wound and encased Dreanen. Flaring into sharp edges, it whirled about him. The light had no difficulty piercing Veen's prison to stir the wind on his face.

"Hold!" a woman yelled. Bernie? She stood at the edge of the lawn with a quarterstaff in her hands.

Gbad'Wu soundlessly rushed Dreanen from the opposite direction. Her spear struck his wrist with its blade, shearing off a sliver of the metal where it hit the light. Unharmed, Dreanen drew back from the monk.

Small as she was, dressed in black linens bound by cloth strips, Gbad'Wu moved with more grace and agility than even the varrow had. Her necklaces, now in black, blues, and purples, moved with her.

"If you can break his spell, hurry, yeah? He's got an army of wights in the temple."

Gbad'Wu's face grew more determined. She held up a hand to stall Bernie's approach and positioned herself between Veen and the mage. "Then I warn you," she said, picking up the broken point of her spear. "Without surrender, this will not end well for you."

"You're no spellbreaker," Dreanen said with a laugh. "Do your worst."

"Oui," Gbad'Wu replied. The monk flung the metal shard at him. With a flicker, it vanished into his enchantment. "Yet I see your armor is not quite as bright now."

The glow swelled around Dreanen's hand and flashed forward. Gbad'Wu sidestepped his strike easily and raised her spear. His hand cracked the staff of the spear, splitting the wood in two. She dodged another jab and lobbed the end of her staff at him. Dreanen flinched, throwing him off balance. Gbad'Wu struck with the spear's blade. It sparked as the light slowly consumed it.

The mage fell away from her. He cried out in anger as the light shielding him dimmed more. Dreanen swiped wildly for Gbad'Wu's leg but missed.

Her face, a plane of certainty, never goaded the necromancer.

But Veen's hatred fed on the man's struggle. "He has the Heart of Rethfor, Gbad'Wu," Veen said, staring at the velvet sack trapped behind the mage's belt.

Dreanen chuckled. "I wouldn't waste it."

Gbad'Wu choked up on the end of her broken staff, flipped over the mage, and pressed the spearhead into the light over Dreanen's back. Streaming sparks sprayed out from the screeching metal as it tore. "If you surrender," she said over his whining, "I can make this quick. End your suffering wisely."

The light flickered around him as he rolled away from her. "I do what I must for Lekelith!" Dreanen said, his face shadowed by the hood of his mantle. "After what the war took from me—from them! Yet they refused to fight." The spell resurged around him, brightening.

Gathering at his fingertips, the light spiked from his right hand. He lunged at Gbad'Wu. The point of his swipe connected below her breast. Without a sound, beads fell from her necklace before she hit the ground.

"Bastard!" Veen yelled. "I'll scatter your bones to the four corners!" Smashing himself against the air, Veen growled and singed the grass with Nelis's blade.

Dreanen grimaced as the light drained from the spike and enveloped him again. Though a thin shell of what it had been, the light made Bernie flinch when the mage strode her way.

Bernie raised a hand before her and stumbled back. A silver glint reflected the approaching spell from her lowered staff. She'd bound Dundy's buckle to the weapon. "Bernie! Take up your arms, woman! He murdered Dundy!" And Nelis.

The blaze of Lekelithian anger streaked her cheeks. Dreanen, who had bothered to look back at Veen, didn't see her swing. A screech accompanied the shearing of the buckle. The staff snapped. But it had worked. The glow left Dreanen as he tottered sideways. Bernie kicked his knee, bringing him down, before her meaty fist punched his cheek.

The air released Veen. He scrambled to his feet. Nelis's sword roasted the misty air.

Bernie wiggled her hand about and picked up her quarterstaff, trimmed to a point. She positioned herself to run Dreanen through. Dreanen shouted. Bernie sailed back ten feet and landed prone.

"You!" Dreanen said to Veen. "Your time—"

The world silenced when Gbad'Wu's hand grabbed a fistful of Dreanen's hair and jerked him upward. Her knee snapped his jaw in a ruthless blur. Veen dashed forward, leaped onto the wet grass at the necromancer's side, and wrenched the velvet sack away from him. The warmth of the Heart permeated it. Bernie sat up and rubbed her neck.

Relieved, but not sated, Veen passed the Heart's container to Gbad'Wu. Raising Nelis's sword, he gripped it with both hands.

"Do not," Gbad'Wu said sternly. She held the wet spot at her side. "He is tied to this undeath and must die. Yet each life you take harms you. Let me carry this burden for Lekelith."

"He killed our kin!"

"And his soul will pay to ferry them elsewhere. But I will not let him take a piece of yours." She stomped her heel on the side of Dreanen's neck. A crack quelled the wailing from the temple. Undead fell where they stood on the lawn. Veen hadn't seen them approaching.

"What scratched you?" Gbad'Wu asked, moving to view his back.

"You shouldn't have done that! He killed my brother!"

Her sympathy stung his eyes. "Then Nelis will find peace in knowing you did not kill—"

Gbad'Wu cut off when Veen jabbed the sword through Dreanen's heart. He spit on the dead mage and kicked him in the gut. But Dreanen hadn't acted alone. He kicked him again. Where had he been heading in his escape? He recognized the manor up the hill. The Boyd Estate.

Heaving clouds in the cool, Bernie joined them. "Where is Dundy, Veen?"

Her gentle voice hurt him more. Without meeting her eye, he

thumbed back to the temple. "Wives' prayer room, upstairs." He grabbed her wrist as she passed. "Get Nelis home, yeah?"

"Ah, now," she moaned sadly.

His feet marched toward the Boyd Estate.

Bernie gasped. "What happened to you?"

"A varrow."

Gbad'Wu ran to his side. "Where are you going?"

His icy stare didn't defeat her concern. "One more piece to this nightmare. I'll see it sorted. Just get Nelis to the Wives."

"Do you need us?" Bernie asked.

Slowing to a brief stop, Veen's gut soured as he wondered how many more children might fall to his father's war. "No. Take our brothers home." Spurred on by his pain, he sprang into a full run.

Chapter 12: Father to Whom

Dead guards sullied the memory of Veen's prank with Elanis in the Boyds' gardens. He marched without caution into the estate.

Splattered blood slickened his steps through the kitchen. If his da had done this, he'd left no witnesses and no evidence of mercy.

An arm lay draped over the banister of the servants' stairs. A boy, twelve years of age at most, had been run through. Dreanen had spoken the truth, but then, the mage had known their father best.

Veen took two stairs at a time. Red drops trailed out to the residence and over to the next wing. Candelabra shone upon his da's next victims. Guards this time. Veen bolted up a sweeping staircase.

On the dim fourth story, a wide-eyed, fair-haired woman lay on a floral rug. A stab wound darkened her dressing gown over her belly. Her breath strained as she mouthed silent threats at him and clutched her wound. He dodged her arm.

A muffled cry froze him. A child's cry.

Swaying in a faint breeze, the bedchamber door rested slightly ajar. With a black steel dagger in one hand and Nelis's short sword in the other, Veen kicked it open.

Aside from small details, half of the room reflected a mirror image of the other. Two twin four-poster beds occupied the center of the chamber, larger than his home in Teallaigh Te. At the far end, curtains lost the breeze and fell to reveal his father, who had hefted the end of a trunk onto the windowsill. His da jerked around and spotted Veen. Cries came from inside the trunk.

Shame flickered over his da's face before he barked, "Get out, Little Stille! This is no place for you!"

In the hours that had passed, Veen had grown to hate his own name. The sword heated to white as he strode in. "What malevolent fae have you captured in that trunk, Da?"

Near the engraved walnut beds, something smelled stale. Dark splotches stained the blanket topping the bed on his left. Veen reached for it.

"Don't, Little Stille!" His da drew a dagger and pointed the blade at Veen while balancing the trunk. "Don't do it, son!"

Veen gave the bedding a tug. His eyes ran from the blood-soaked body of a boy to his da's wincing face. "How? How can you murder children?"

With a tug, his da hauled the trunk in from the sill, letting it crash to the floor. He unlatched the curved metal handle. "They're not children, Stille. They're your enemy! They'll grow to spit on your children in the streets. Or worse, turn Lekelith into Merith. You want our kin wearing chains and collars, do you?" His da's hand reached into the trunk and brought out a dark-haired girl. She squirmed to be free of the hand squeezing her dressing gown at her nape. He seized her face to muffle her cries and held her against him.

Nelis's blade cooled when his da put his dagger to her throat. Blood dripped from the blade to her gown.

"You're not, are you?" Veen asked the girl. "You're just a wee girleen—"

"Shut your mouth and turn away, Stille!" his da shouted.

Nelis's blade brightened to the red of a young sunset. Veen took a step toward them. "You've been suckling at Mad Ferra's tit, Da. You're supposed to protect children! You nurture them to keep them from becoming their parents. To make them better, like Nelis did for me, yeah?"

"How dare you? I watched over you boys!"

"Did you now? Leave us coin and meat and clothes and medicine?" Veen took another step. "No, you didn't. Nelis had to see to that. We stole in Aontus what our neighbors couldn't give, what Master van Echt couldn't spare, Da."

The girl screamed through his fingers as the dagger nicked her neck. "This ugliness protects the lowlanders! I protect youse!"

"No! You don't!" Veen lunged closer. "You and your necromancer. Youse lied about the Filii Cinere taking the lowlanders for slaves. Youse killed and enslaved them!"

Emboldened by his father's flexing jaw, Veen took another step and held the heat of the enchanted blade away from him. "You used the children of your fallen brethren as fodder for your army. Dundy and Tabbi and Skitter."

"That Tabbi should have kept her mouth shut; we didn't want to take a Wife. But I heard what she told you. A mage would've figured it out soon enough."

"And Nelis?"

Maintaining his grip on the girl's face, his da lowered his dagger to his side and straightened. "What are you on about?"

"Dreanen. He killed him. He tried to kill us both." Veen showed his da the varrow's handiwork.

His father's face didn't register remorse for more than a second before he shook his head. "Doesn't matter, Little Stille. With the Heart, he can undo it."

Veen risked two steps. Too far. The dagger met her throat again. "Or he'd turn Aontus into his own army against Racine. He said as much when he refused to stop the spell from taking Nelis."

The elder Stille raised his eyebrows. "He wouldn't. He's like my son."

Veen's chest chilled. "He's dead."

His da hung his head. Real remorse. For the son he had chosen or for his failed plan?

"Why couldn't you stay in the grave, Da? This obsession . . . Because of you, I lost my whole family."

His da seemed confused. "'Tisn't too late for Nelis, Stille. And the others. We just need a mage. Son, believe me; we weren't going to take Aontus as a weapon. This was just about tonight. The lowlanders need to see they're not safe! Don't look at me like that! Not with her eyes."

"End it here, Da. Let the sweet girl go."

"You shouldn't have interfered, Stille."

Veen tightened his grip. "Because the people will know you're no martyr? That you won't let their peace grow? You sink ships. You burn buildings. You free prisoners. And you murder? You murder children! Do you even see it? You hide in the shadows when you should go to the feckin' council!"

Denial formed in his father's eyes. "Trust them? Their kind—"

"You're just an infection, plaguing the lowlanders."

"I am still your father!"

Veen saw Nelis in his father's anger and despised it. "My da doesn't murder wee girls! Ma would never let you do this. Neither will your real sons."

Squeezed tighter, the girl whined and released more tears. His da's gaze dropped to her braids. After two breaths, he let his dagger fall to the carpet.

Veen's fingers caught his da's attention as they beckoned for the girl.

Backing away, the murderer lifted his arms in surrender before turning to the window. Running past Veen, the girl wailed. Her cries faded down the corridor.

"Maybe you're right," his da said. "Iona saw it. I could see it. Youse were better off without me. And I found Dreanen, a boy himself, hurt by the war. Alone. I figured a magus is as good as ten men in a fight." Master Stille van Veen, supposed hero, wept and sagged against the wall next to the window. "We need to get out of here while we still have each other."

"I never had you," Veen said. "I meant what I said; you took away the only father I've known." The denial returned to his da's eyes, giving Veen all the permission he needed. One swift thrust. The white blade sliced through the lowlander armor without resistance. "Let them know what you really are. Ma does." Veen ripped it free. Tears coursed down his cheeks. The sword sizzled and scorched away the blood.

Veen sheathed his blades, put the medallion in his mouth, and straddled the windowsill. But his hand refused to release and let him fall. Staring down at the gardens, he considered what it'd mean for a lowlander to be found responsible for so many deaths, instead of a crazed magus of the upper sort. He climbed back inside.

Veen's voice croaked as he uttered into his father's ear, "I'm not doing this for you." Hefting the man, he managed to get them both on the windowsill.

Blowing over his medallion, he dropped out of the window. It was harder than he had imagined. Carrying the weight of his father and staving off the searing pain in his back exhausted his breath too quickly. Veen decided he was close enough and released the body.

When his feet lighted, a figure dashed forward from the garden. He drew Nelis's sword before he recognized Gbad'Wu.

She displayed a couple of snapped branches with clusters bobbing at the ends. "Rowan berries. Let us get you to the cart where I can salve the varrow's poison."

Irritated he'd now have to explain his da's body, he said, "I told you to take my brother home."

Gbad'Wu put her wrist on her hip. "I do not answer to you." Then she laid the berries on his da's belly and knelt to grab his legs.

"What are you doing?" Veen asked. "You're hurt."

"We both are."

Voices from above reached them, though no one had come to the window yet.

"I suggest we go now. Tout de suite!"

They managed only half of the lawn to the temple before needing to rest. "Who is he?" Gbad'Wu asked through her panting.

"A terrible goat of a man," Veen answered. His lips trembled. "My da."

Her brown eyes fell to the man before she tilted her head.

He stalled her from speaking. "I don't need comforting. And he's not going back to Teallaigh Te. I'd have left him, if the lowlanders wouldn't have paid the price."

"This was his doing?" she asked. "The temple too?"

Nodding, Veen put his hand to his back and quickly retracted it. "I don't know where to leave him."

Gbad'Wu thought before taking his father by the knees again. "We do not have long. Is there a passage to the necropolis in this temple?"

"Aye."

"Then that is our answer," she said.

He hefted the elder van Veen before she was ready and fell back to his knees, sucking in air through his teeth.

"Mais, Veen . . . we make it dignified. Let it be more than he deserves."

Back at the temple, Bernie had enshrouded Nelis and Dundy in some of the gray cloaks. As Veen began undoing Nelis's shroud, he explained, "We found this old man outside and thought it best if we leave him here. I'll wrap him in this. Nelis won't mind. He'll get proper pelts when we get to Teallaigh Te, yeah? Yes."

There in the catacombs, Veen left his da tucked behind the ancient fallen and wrapped in the garb of his enemy. Chewing the inside of his cheek, he didn't say anything else until Bernie had driven them out of Aontus on Master van Echt's cart.

With Nelis's hand in his, he let Gbad'Wu mash the berries and spread them onto his wounds. "You will feel relief soon."

She spoke the truth. In a matter of breaths, the inferno under his skin had passed, though the pain remained. His mind, trying to make sense of the night, spilled his thoughts out of his mouth. Bernie nearly turned the cart around when she heard Tabbi had been left behind.

"No," Gbad'Wu said. "A varrow would leave little for us to gather. We must find solace in knowing her fate."

"How do you know so much about those beasties?" Veen asked.

"They are what led me to the monastery," she answered, wiping her hands on her legs. "I offer you a deal. You share the whole story of what happened tonight, and I will tell you of my escape from the varrows, oui?"

His eyes rose to Bernie, who remained focused on the road ahead. Embarrassed to admit what his father had become, he tried to console himself with the reminder his ma was still a hero, the real champion of Teallaigh Te. The women always seemed to be. He squeezed Nelis's hand. "Agreed, if Bernie agrees to protect the Heart of Rethfor and not return it to the feckin' temple."

Chapter 13: Safe Hands

Veen came back to the present when Gbad'Wu set Dreanen's sack at the base of his stool. She had been splitting her time between sitting with Bernie and him as the Wives prepared their brothers' bodies in separate alcoves of the catacombs within Mount Noafa. Cleaned and dressed in white linen, Nelis honestly did appear to be sleeping on the pelts covering the raised slab.

"He wasn't even armed," Veen mumbled.

Gbad'Wu squinted and shook her head for an explanation.

"I've killed more than a handful of men, Gbad'Wu," he said. "Fifteen, if I'm honest. Clarkson sends our band in to clean up problems before they get out of hand. When they do . . . I've killed to defend my friends, once to defend myself. To save my brother's soul. But the fifteenth . . . 'twas murder."

"Come with me to the Mount, Veen. Train in the shelter of the monastery."

He frowned at her. "You think I'm broken now?"

"I ask you to consider it. If you wish to go, I am leaving tomorrow after the services."

"Tomorrow? That's rather soon, no?"

She looked behind them. "It will not be long before the theft of the Heart is discovered."

One more choice where all the options felt incomplete. "You should get some rest," he said. "The lowlanders are in your debt. Lekelith is, even if it doesn't know it. If 'tweren't for you, that bastard would've gotten away with the relic. He'd have started another war."

She took the stool next to him. "And if you had not sent for me? And if Nelis had not hidden it away? And if even Mage Curtiss had not hired you to steal it? And if, and if." Her hand reached over his shoulder, bringing with it the welcome scent of hyacinth. "The connections between our actions and those around us are not easily separated. Many of my people—the Daijon—believe the gods beat their drums and we dance to their rhythm.

"That never felt right to me. Many of our choices are too challenging to say we follow along like in a play." Her arm withdrew, taking her fingers to the beads over her bosom. "You honored your family and chose to guard the Heart. Could that kind of decision tear so deeply if it were fate?"

He blinked away his tears.

"Be bold in your tenets, and the world rests in safe hands," Gbad'Wu repeated.

Wife Julienne appeared with a limestone circle in her arms. Laying the blank memory wheel at Nelis's feet, she asked Veen, "Would you care for some tea?" Three other Wives came behind her with a cot and provisions for Veen to stay until they swaddled Nelis in pelts for the funeral.

"Nah, Wife Julienne," Veen managed, taking her hand, warm to the fingertips. "Thank you for all you've done."

She bowed her head. "'Twas nothing. We will give you privacy to clean yourself." She turned to Gbad'Wu. "Perhaps now would be a good time to tend to that wound you've been hiding, child?"

With Veen and Wife Julienne silently opposing her, Gbad'Wu relented. "Oui, perhaps it would."

Three mallets and chisels joined the limestone wheel before they left him and Nelis alone. Taking up Dreanen's sack, Veen noticed its weight. They'd hidden the Heart in The Wayward Tulip's cellar. What else had the mage taken?

He reached in and lifted free the mulberry-purple tome. Sinking onto the cot, Veen flipped it open. Were wights the only way one could return to Cyr from the Glades? Expelling malevolent spirits. He turned the page. Bones of protection. A drawing of a dog's innards. Three pages flipped by. A bloody handprint, centered on an otherwise blank page, ended his search. He could hear Elanis telling him, "You can put pickles in a trifle; it doesn't mean you should." Focused on his brother, he closed the tome and concealed it inside the sack. Nelis would never forgive him for taking this kind of risk, even if it ended well.

Scooting Nelis's feet aside, Veen hopped his buttocks up to the red deer pelts. He ran his fingers over the grainy circle. The Wives had already chiseled lines dividing the memorial into seven equal sections, one for each of Nelis's dearest, friend or family.

Deciding easily on what Oren would chisel, Veen picked up the tools and set to work on a plate of oysters and ale. When he was satisfied that he could convincingly explain what he'd carved, he pondered the next section. "What would you and Joseb remember most, boy?"

"Making my life difficult," a sad voice said. Elanis's shoulders drooped when she spotted Nelis. Her jaw trembled before she smacked her lips.

Veen slid the circle off his lap, got up, and fell against her.

"Gbad'Wu sent word. I got here as quickly as I could. I'm sorry, Veen. So sorry. The others had already left Racine."

He hugged her tight.

"Gbad'Wu was right the other night, you know?" she said, running her fingers through his hair. "If I'm allowed to be contrite, he deserved great credit. You are a legacy to be proud of."

"I've made an awful fool of him, then."

"Never." She kissed the top of his head. Then her fingers explored the stone. "I could give you a litany of contradictions to your nonsense but would prefer if you'd assume reason on your own and allow me to add to the wheel. An unguent for grief, I hope." Thankful to do one less carving, he let her work on one side and took up another hammer and chisel for the other.

"I see you've added the inveterate ale and oysters," she said, conjuring Veen's smile. "You'll not want to forget his stomach's reaction to soft cheeses."

"Ach, no! I can't put that on a memory wheel, El."

"You're sure?" she teased. "That could be Joseb's contribution." Adjusting her spectacles, she grinned.

"Stop trying to make me laugh."

"All right," she said softly. "Why don't you let me work on this while you have a bath. I see they've brought you food. Do you mind sharing? I'm famished."

"Sure." After splitting an apple, he tore the bread and slathered on some of the rowan-berry jelly Bernie had insisted he eat upon hearing of Gbad'Wu's cure. While she ate, he bathed. The water had gone cold but soothed him.

Returning to Nelis's side, he bit into his half of the apple, which didn't taste much like anything at all, and took in Elanis's handiwork. Two angry figures exchanged rude gestures while a smaller figure slumped behind them. Thus started a fit of laughter they shared until Veen began hammering in Teague's memory. The mirth left him quickly.

"I'm not entirely sure what Teague would leave," he admitted. A snicker broke free, anticipating a lewd suggestion from Elanis.

"The bow," she answered. "Definitely the bow." Elanis caressed Nelis's hand. For his ears, she said, "Teague and I spent hours hunting down the one artificer in all of Barask who was skilled enough to enchant it." She petted Nelis's forearm through the linen. "That was the morning after their first night together."

"That was months ago. No, a year." Veen wished he could demand a real reason for being kept in the dark. "You've known since then?"

Elanis nodded. "Smitten kittens." Her snicker drooped. Addressing Nelis again, she said, "He'll find out by letter. I'm so very sorry, Nelis, but it was the best I could do. Oren and Joseb will see Teague right."

While Veen did his best to carve the lines of the recurve bow in the limestone, Elanis busied herself with her mantle. The shimmery silver material tore fairly evenly in a three-inch strip across the bottom. She tied the scrap around Nelis's waist like a knight's belt. "Tawdry and flamboyant for him, but I need him to know we were friends. When he sees this in the Glades—"

"He's keenly aware of his family, Elanis."

Gently placing Nelis's hand on the pelts, she wiped her cheeks. "Right. You get some rest and let me cry in peace."

"I haven't—"

"Don't make me call you Runt."

"I won't, El. I promise. But I need to add my own memory to the wheel first." And so he did. Then he moved aside the sack with the varrow-hide tome, lay on the cot, and drifted off.

A hand rocked his shoulder, waking him from a nightmare. Sleep had taken him deep into a horrid dream. All he could see was his father's face when he woke. He bolted upright in a panic. Upon seeing Elanis, the real nightmare came back to him. "They haven't wrapped him yet, have they?"

"No," Wife Julienne answered from behind Elanis. "But this is the second morning; we will shortly. Master van Echt and Master Mann have provided the final hart pelts we needed. Between Dundy and Nelis, to say we were in short supply would be—"

"Hilarious," Elanis interrupted.

Giving Elanis a tolerant look, Wife Julienne glided around the slab. "'Tis time to say your farewells, Little Stille."

When he stood, Elanis turned to go as well. "El," he said, "will you say the Hook's bit?" He forced a steady breath. "I don't think I can."

She nodded, gave Nelis a backhanded slap on the leg, and left with a final sad smile for his brother.

After taking up the brass shield, Veen laid it on Nelis's chest. "I owed you more, yeah?" He rested his elbows on the pelts. "Who knows, maybe I am your legacy? Or maybe I can be? I will make you proud, brother."

Veen waved Wife Julienne into the alcove. Once the pelts covered Nelis's face, Veen tucked the short sword behind his belt and took up the velvet sack. In the sanctuary, Bernie and Elanis stood on the hearth's steps, beneath the Wives surrounding the brazier. The entirety of Teallaigh Te had assembled below them. Friendly faces pained by loss were too difficult to acknowledge. Veen found Gbad'Wu in her pink silks again and aimed for her.

At her side, he said, "You tested me with that tome."

"It was unintentional; je promets. I did not consider the temptation until I saw Elanis in the Tulip." She bumped him with her shoulder. "And what have you decided to do with the tome?"

Veen searched her brown eyes for an answer. "I haven't. My gut says to destroy it."

"Mais?"

He directed her attention to Elanis. "In the right hands, it could reveal a weakness in those dark arts." Could they even retake the Caperis' islands? He mumbled, "Dare to think it."

Gbad'Wu surprised him by saying, "Good." She pointed her chin at Elanis. "You trust her with it?"

"With it. With my soul, so I do. She wouldn't so much as touch the Heart for fear of . . ." He recalled the countless arguments between Elanis and Joseb over sorcery. "Well, losing control."

The crowd fell silent as Wife Julienne, now wearing her formal flame-colored vestment, climbed the hearth to stand between Elanis and Bernie. She combined her fists under her bosom and bowed her head, signaling the town elders to bring out the deceased.

Dundy's girth proved too much for the stairs of the hearth, requiring them to lay him and Nelis at the bottom. Veen chewed the inside of his lip to stave off his tears. But the sound of Elanis's solemn voice tipped the scales against him.

"We have a tradition in the Hook," she explained. "When one of our own has fallen, we recite a passage in hopes it eases their passing. Many mercenaries do not have family and friends to wish them farewell. I am—we are heartened to see that is not the case for Nelis, our redoubtable friend and brother.

"Brothers and sisters of the Hook," Elanis said, "we have lost a member. His reasons for joining remain his own. The sacrifice Nelis van Veen has made garners our humility. May he find peace in order to start anew."

With a nod to Wife Julienne, Elanis stepped back in line. "Rethfor's hearth is open to more than his faithful in the Glades," Wife Julienne began. Veen didn't hear much else of what she said, his mind preoccupied with the bound red deer pelts under the brass shield. Then Master van Echt and the other elders lifted Nelis and Dundy to carry them down to their graves.

Although Wife Julienne had offered the catacombs, Veen wanted Nelis near their ma. He'd been touched when Bernie had asked if Dundy could join them.

Even the weather participated in the ceremony as they descended Mount Noafa. Nelis had loved these sunny, crisp mornings. Two openings interrupted the grass at the edge of the meadow. Just beyond them, a yew tree sapling, a gift from the elders, swayed in the breeze of its new home. The men held Nelis and Dundy aloft until the villagers had gathered in a semicircle. Then they lowered them inside.

Bernie approached the graves and tossed in rings of tulips and poppies that matched those in her auburn hair. Without hesitation, she sang out the first line of Nelis's favorite song, "Birte Foley." They had agreed to share the song; Dundy had enjoyed it, too, and Bernie didn't think she'd hold her voice steady for two songs.

Those who knew the song joined in. When it was over, Veen vacantly watched the procession of well-wishers deposit fistfuls of dirt in the graves and depart for the fire Master van Echt had built.

Veen ended the line behind Bernie and released his damp soil on Nelis's shield. Bernie sniffled more rapidly when they both dropped a handful for Dundy. She sat cross-legged next to his grave, while Masters Selke and Barrow shoveled.

Gbad'Wu ran her fingers over his da's wheel while she spoke with Elanis. Not wanting to think about his da, he stood still, staring at the home Nelis had given him and the life he'd wanted for Veen. But that had been a life to live together.

Master van Echt shouted for him to join the gathering at the fire. While he cooked the venison, the deer that had provided the pelts, Master van Echt told Veen tales no one else knew about Nelis. Things the elder had needed to throw a little weight around to cover. The type of things that had kept them alive through the harshest winters. They laughed briefly over a few of his failed thefts and childish schemes. Veen's exhaustion muddled his mind with laughter and tears.

The Manns overheard the last tale. "Now you do know I killed one of the deer?" Master Mann said, leering at the barrels of ale someone had carried over from the Tulip. Master van Echt shook his head until the pik turned and smoothly changed to nodding. "Happy to do it for Nelis. Happy not to do it for you, too, you know what I mean?"

"Yes, yes," Mrs. Mann cawed. The elderly pik pulled her arm free of her husband's. "You did well. Now give me some time with our young Master van Veen. Walk with me." Hand in hand, he and his first midwife reached the dry-stone wall at the road's edge. "Pull your hood up, dear. This cold wind will bring you as many maladies as an itching ship wench."

He did as she said, though the breeze was more refreshing than cold, and looked down at her when she took his hand again. Soft and wrinkled. She rubbed her thumbs over the back of his hand as she spoke. "In my . . . gods, nearly three hundred years, I've seen more grief than one heart should. People will tell you how to grieve if you let them. Don't, Little Stille.

Your heart must mend itself. 'Twill hurt and take time, possibly years."

One of her hands left his for a moment to fix her shawl over her thin white hair. She returned it and said, "The world is open to you, and Teallaigh Te is not moving." Unsure what she was saying, he scratched his stubble. "Don't get stuck in the bog, boy. No one with half a mind wants that for you."

He knelt to her height, his knee dipping into soft mud. Pulling her woolen shawl forward, he tried to tell her he'd made up his mind to go, but couldn't without his lips quivering.

Mrs. Mann patted his face and wiped away the tears. Her silvery eyes beckoned a hug. When he obliged, she kissed his cheek.

Ever faithful, Master Mann came running back to her side. "You may be short Little Stille," the pik said, "but not so short to be coming after our women, so."

Mrs. Mann giggled before grasping her husband's hand. "We're too old to dance for Nelis," she said. "But believe me, I'll have it done right."

"And we'll drink for him! Two pints!" Master Mann added before receiving a reluctant agreement from his wife. She trailed behind her husband's sprint for the barrels.

Bernie said something to Gbad'Wu and struck off toward town. With Elanis discussing Master van Echt's cooking, he thought he might as well give the monk his decision. She acknowledged his approach and inclined her head toward his home. Rather than enter, she took a seat on the small step up to the door. Veen sat next to her. The men were still refilling the graves.

"Not to sound like the sun shines out of my arse," he said, "but I suspected you were here for me. Prayed I was wrong, but the fae blood curse of the lowlanders, it knows. I hope I don't offend by saying that; no one wants to feel broken." But, yes, looking around, his world felt darker.

"I take no offense," she said seriously. "I have my pupil in Hibernia, my gift back to the lowlanders. Whereas you, my dear Veen, will certainly be trained by Ukresti herself."

He sniffed. "Is that a good thing? I haven't actually committed yet. I could change my mind."

"Having been her pupil, I honestly cannot say."

Her expression did not reveal a joke. "Aye, well, if it all goes to the high ground, Rethfor should be guarding my back. He owes me, doesn't he?"

"Careful," she said. "I cannot tell you why, but the world has challenges ahead. We may need those favors."

A patch of sunlight moved across the field beyond the graves and lit on the Manns' wattle-and-daub house. "If Teallaigh Te winds up with you and Hibernia as its guardians," Gbad'Wu continued, "so be it. But I suspect your path is longer."

"How can you be sure 'twasn't to protect the Heart?"

She held her palms out. "I have no explanation to give. If you require it, I understand." She leaned in to look him in the eye. "Do you? I do not believe so. Not a man who finds meaning in counting birds." Her smile warmed him, then pained him; he should have known. "Let us eat. That venison smells wonderful. And we will need the energy; our journey to the southern Asdales starts soon."

"The southern Asdales? By the Cloud?"

"Exciting, no?" Bernie asked. Rebellion splint mail covered her torso where two sacks draped, plump with necessities for a long journey. She drove her new quarterstaff hard into the mud and leaned against it. "Dishonored," she said, giving the armor a rap with her knuckles, "the way it was used when last we saw it. I hope you don't mind."

"'Tis a salve for my heart, seeing you in that," Veen said. A true hero of Lekelith. "I only wish my ma could see you."

Bernie looked up to the sky. "She has the best view, Veen."

The half-moon hung low in the clear sky. There, in the green Glades running across its surface, he knew Nelis and his ma had reunited. He tried to feel comforted by that.

"Where is the Heart now?" he asked Bernie.

She thrust her right hip against her simple burlap sack. "May make the trip more interesting than it should, but safest with us, I think."

Gbad'Wu led them over to where the others had begun the celebration for Nelis and Dundy. Teallaigh Te cheered and drank to their brothers.

Elanis eyed Bernie and asked, "Why do I feel a journey looming?" Gbad'Wu tilted her head for Veen to answer. "What?"

"C'mere," he said. Veen explained his decision to go to the Mount. "Anyroads, that girleen may recall 'Little Stille' being in her chamber. Best for Teallaigh Te if I go for a while."

The news diminished her appetite, though Elanis said, "I guess we can't fight change, can we?"

"No. But the Filii Cinere are dead. Suppose there's solace in that."

Elanis didn't seem convinced. "Best to stay vigilant there. They are known now. And Ameera is already weaving webs throughout her empire to snare them. She doesn't have 'resources' here, but if I know her, she's procuring them as we speak."

"There's more, El." After telling her of the necromancer's tome and his hopes for it, he waited.

Oddly enough, she began eating again. With a finger to her mouth, she chewed. "Firstly, I'm quite confident a book bound in varrow hide should be called a 'grimoire' at a minimum. Secondly, yes, I think I can get away with working on that. My new position—thank you, Nelis, you beautiful liar—affords me a private chamber in the Tower and far more—I'm not exaggerating, far more—leniency than the archivists." A slow fire of excitement spread in her eyes.

"And one more wee thing," he said slowly.

"No need to cajole; ask away."

He presented Nelis's sword. "Can you see that Teague gets this? I thought I would give him the bow, but returning a gift feels awful rude." Veen fingered the handle. "Tell him it avenged Nelis."

"Of course."

"Oh!" Veen said, stricken with a sickening thought. "The Fuchs—"

"Are safe and sound," Elanis finished. "I inquired on my way here. One of their servants swore gray was not Lady Fuchs's color, 'perish the thought!'" After he slid the scabbard behind her belt, she shoved her platter under his nose. "Now eat."

He accepted a honeyed bap and confessed, "I don't know if I can do this."

With her mouth full, she nudged him. "Keep this in mind. If you fail, you'll have to live in a trunk in my chamber. I can't swim over here every day." She stared over the edge of her spectacles until he grinned. "You do realize, Joseb will hound you to no end for the secrets you learn?"

"Aye, just him," Veen said, relieved to have her endorsement for his decision, even if he needed to stand on his own now. "I love you, El."

She elbowed his shoulder and looked away. "I'm still considering calling you Runt, you know? For his sake."

"You'll do what you think is best, yeah?"

A hand tugged at his sleeve. "Excuse me, child," a young pik Wife said up to him. He turned to find her, another Wife, and Wife Julienne behind him.

Wife Julienne passed Nelis's memory wheel to Veen, as the other human Wife handed Dundy's to Bernie. "When you are ready, Little Stille."

With everyone watching, Veen suddenly forgot how to walk on his own two feet. So he intently studied the wheel as he went. A field of Patevian poppies had filled in the final section. Bernie. The memory of playing in the very meadow next to them stung his heart. Smiling, he pressed the circle firmly and evenly into the soil and bent. "I love you, brother." Veen kissed the thatched home he'd chiseled into the limestone. "I will make you proud."

Chapter 14: Omens

With their travels taking them through Trône d'Argent, Veen convinced Elanis to leave Teallaigh Te earlier than expected. "We're going on foot?" she asked as they left the Tulip.

Gbad'Wu waved her arm toward the rolling hills. "Mais oui! It is the best way to see the world."

"I'll remember to clarify before agreeing to your adventures in the future."

Veen adjusted Nelis's bow on his shoulder. "That doesn't mean we're hoofing it all the way to the Asdales, no? Surely not."

Bernie didn't seem keen, either.

Laughing, Gbad'Wu winked. "Sadly, no. We have work to do. We will catch a boat downriver in Virtud Luz."

At the wooden bridge crossing the river Eagna, they met their first fellow traveler, an older man with white straggly hair. Bottles clinked in the crates stacked on his horse's cart.

"Hail there, my good people," the man said, raising his hand. "If youse are going to Aontus, youse'll be wantin' to buy a bottle of my remedy."

"Remedy?" Elanis asked. "Remedy for what?"

"Well," the man said, bringing his horse to a stop, "Lenny's Tonic is a near-perfect panacea. I say near perfect because the good stuff won't cure your debt." He released a rehearsed cackle. "And with the undead problems in the capital, youse'd best keep a bottle close."

"What?" Bernie asked incredulously.

"Youse heard me right. Lenny's Tonic saved the city from a hoard of undead the night before last. Sad shame it couldn't bring them back to life, but it put them down lightning fast!"

Elanis snorted. "Your selling point is 'my tonics will kill the undead?'"

Sensing he was losing his sale to Elanis, Lenny focused in on Bernie. "Handy if you've got a cough, handy if you've got any unwelcomed visitors in the night, miss."

Before he realized her intent, Bernie had butted her quarterstaff against the bottom of the crates and used her weight to slide a stack over the side of the bridge. They crashed into the river with a racket.

"You mad cow!" the charlatan roared. He leaped to protect the remaining crates on the cart. "This is medicine!"

Bernie's staff smashed his hand against the cart. "Selling piss water to folks who don't know any better, yeah? Scaring them into it, are you? Not in my town, you don't!" A low sweep of her weapon knocked him down. He clung to the side of the cart. Her staff prodded his breastbone until he lay flat on the bridge's planks.

His eyes pleaded for interference from the others. Gbad'Wu visibly fought her laughter when the second stack crashed into the water.

Bernie led the horse off the bridge, turned it around, and aimed it at Aontus. She spanked the steed and roared, causing them all to jump. Hopeful they were getting a ride, Veen was disappointed when the cart cracked and snapped as it bounded out of sight.

With her staff crooked in her elbow, Bernie allowed the charlatan to stand. Climbing the bridge rails, he bent over and searched for his tonics in the depths. "What madness do you suffer? That was my livelihood, woman!"

"'Tis a narrow river, but a deep one," Bernie said. "I'd wager you could catch them before they hit bottom." She grabbed his ankles and heaved. His shouting was silenced. The shout returned when he surfaced and splashed about. "No such luck, no? Well, do enjoy your stroll away from my village." The threat in her voice made Veen wonder if she planned to make them escort the man.

Gbad'Wu giggled and led on. "This journey will be amusing."

After some time, the monk tapped Veen's shoulder and pointed to a stone wall where two magpies picked at a dead mouse. "Two for joy, yes?" He nodded. "Très bien. We've a long way to go. But first . . ." She sighed longingly. "Scallops."

Other Books in the Lamentation's End series:

THANK YOU FOR READING!

IF YOU ENJOYED *TENETS*, PLEASE WRITE A REVIEW.
YOUR ENCOURAGING WORDS BRIGHTEN MY DAY
AND INSPIRE ME TO CONTINUE SHARING MORE
TALES FROM CYR.

About the Author

Wade Lewellyn-Hughes is an author, screenwriter, and general creative based in Montana. Aiming to bring a vivid world and robust characters to life, he values diversity and differences in this world and the one he's writing.

Sign up for updates on upcoming books and find out more here: http://wadelewellyn.com

www.ingramcontent.com/pod-product-compliance
Lightning Source LLC
Chambersburg PA
CBHW051954170626
46808CB00007B/2619